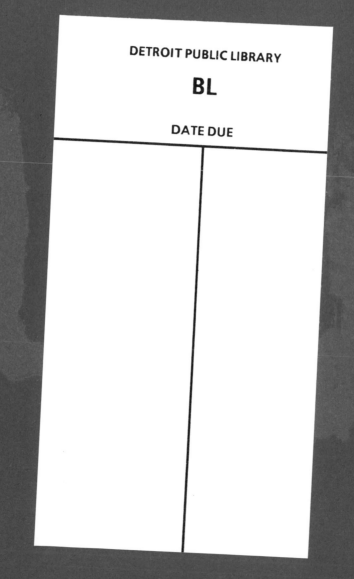

The Impermanence of Heroes

ALSO BY C. F. GRIFFIN

The Impermanence
of Heroes

by C. F. Griffin

CHILTON BOOKS

A Division of Chilton Company Publishers
Philadelphia and New York

To—my mother

The Impermanence of Heroes

Seventeen-year-old Jessica Brewer recalls those days following her eleventh birthday when she and her brother made life bearable for Joe St. George, an embittered Korean War hero and amputee, who had alienated himself from his neighbors.

The day I heard the news was the first Saturday in May; it was a soft, sunny day and it was especially welcome after an endless-seeming spell of cold, gray, drizzly weather. At breakfast time we had to pull the curtains to keep from being dazzled by the sun's path on the sea. After Brock and I did the dishes I went up to make my bed but looked out the window instead of getting to work.

The sky was blue as paint and the water was that deep, impossible color that never seems quite real even when you're looking right at it. The tide was just beginning to come in and the mossers' dories were riding low in the water, heaped with the wet, dark, purple-red seaweed called Irish moss. The men were checking lobster pots on the way in, clearing out the crabs and lobsters and putting in new bait. From the house I couldn't see faces, but I knew who was there by the colors of the floats being tended. J. Wyddyn must have got a big one; I saw him wave it and shout something before pegging its claws and dropping it into the basket at the bottom of the boat. Then he dumped the pink crabs over the side, rebaited the trap, fastened down the lid, and let it slide back into the ocean. Pink crabs are a pest, they eat the bait but aren't worth anything because there's hardly a bit of meat in them.

I felt good all over and the whole world seemed new and shiny as a birthday penny. I hardly ever listen to the surf, any more than I spend time listening to my own heartbeat, but that morning I paused to hear it. Below the foot of the low cliff where our house stands, the waves were breaking far out with a soft crash. At low tide you can see the round rocks that make up the shallow bottom in front of the point. They're all about the same size and their tops are pretty even. Far out near the low-tide mark there is an enormous boulder as big as a small house that sticks out of the water even at high tide; there's another large rock further inshore near the sandbeach that we called the crab rock because it's shaped pretty much like a crab shell and has a flat top. There are a few other largish rocks but the rest are roughly the size of a bushel basket more or less (only round). In between the rocks are innumerable tide-pools floored with smaller rocks and pebbles. The rocks near the low-tide mark have great mops of blackish-brown seaweed growing on them, like dark, coarse heads of hair, and as the waves wash them the seaweed floats up and swirls around, held up by the little air bladders along the strands.

The men finished clearing the traps and began rowing towards the beach, I could hear an oar-lock squeaking, and the rhythmic bump of oars. The men pulled the boats up onto the sand, and, working together, took them up the beach on rollers. The sandpipers rose in a flurry and resumed their prospecting at the water's edge further down the beach. Gulls were wheeling and screeching like rusty hinges and a bunch of them were quarreling over some offal at the high-tide mark on the rocks below the house. Listening more carefully, I could hear the surf sucking and rattling the cobblestones on the other side of the point, and around the point the bell buoy was chiming lazily in the slow swell at the harbor mouth.

Songbirds and robins were twittering and cheeping in the trees to the lee of the house and in the needle-tree (which is really a sort of enormous bush with great long spines on it) in the side yard. Down the street back of the house Mr. Goodfellow's boxer was having hysterics, then I heard the unmistakable knock of George Hopwood's jalopy. Mr. Hopwood is the village printer and his son George delivers the weekly paper every Saturday morning.

Brock was out in the garage tending his mice and I heard his feet on the gravel as he went out to pick up the paper. George called a greeting and went chugging on down the street. There was a long pause; Brock apparently had stopped to read something, then Brock's feet on the gravel path and the back door slammed.

All of a sudden I remembered that I'd better get dressed and make my bed if I wanted to get out into all that sunshine, so I got to it. I put on a bright yellow dress in honor of the day.

When I got halfway down the stairs I saw my mother standing by the living-room picture window looking at the paper, with an odd expression on her face. She looked as if she couldn't make up her mind if she was mad, glad, or sad. When she heard me on the stairs she said, "Jessica?" and glanced up.

"Yes, Mom?"

She waited until I got down the stairs and came towards her, watching me in that way she has, as if she's expecting to go blind tomorrow and feels she has to store up everything she sees for remembering later. It bothers some people, but I'm used to it. She always looks a little abstracted when she does it, and she always has to hesitate a moment and shift gears before she's seeing you the way other people do. I waited and she blinked, then said, "It says here that Joe St. George is dead."

"Oh." It took a moment for the news to sink in. I was looking at the *Mackerel Cove Defender* wrongside up, but I could read the headline, and, indeed, that was what it said.

"May God have mercy on his soul."

I looked at her to see if she was kidding, she says things like that and sometimes it's hard to tell if she means them or not. She wasn't kidding, she meant it. And somehow that phrase pretty well summed it up, how I felt too just at that moment, I mean. I waited for her to tell me the rest.

She was scanning the paper. "It says he died of wounds received during the Korean 'police action.' Apparently his spine never healed properly. There's a list of medals as long as your arm; did you know he was in the second wave on Omaha Beach in World War II and got a D.S.C. with oak leaf clusters?"

"Brock and I saw it. He kept a handful of medals in the same drawer as the can opener. One time Joe said that you only get a D.S.C. for being killed, but that

4

they'd given it to him very prematurely. I remember because back then I had to come home and look up 'prematurely' in the dictionary."

"He was a bitter man."

It's not like my mother to write someone off with a cliché. I asked myself why she'd said that. The obvious answer was that she was giving me an out, sealing off the conversation with an unarguable truth so I could drop it if I wanted to. Sometimes she's too considerate, because she makes you think when maybe you'd rather not. I thought back to that phrase she'd used earlier and realized it was familiar because in British whodunits it's part of the formula the judges use in pronouncing death sentences, only they say, "May God have mercy on *your* soul," because they're talking to the prisoner, not about him.

I tried to read my mother's expression but there are times when her face is blank as a cat's, and right then was one of them. I almost asked her if she knew or had guessed what had really happened five years ago, but after keeping the secret all that time it was as if it had rusted shut and I couldn't have talked about it to anyone but my brother if I'd wanted to. And I hadn't made up my mind then if I wanted to. I asked, "Where's Brock?" I'd have to tell him the news if he hadn't seen it already, and I wanted to talk to him about it.

"With his mice, I think. Wear a jacket if you go out, it's colder than it looks."

I went out by way of the kitchen, taking my jacket off the peg in the back entry as I passed, and down the wooden steps into the back yard. Donald the duck came quacking out of the bushes back of the tool shed (which isn't used as a tool shed and used to be a playhouse

5

when we were little; we still use it to keep things in).
She came waddling over to me, her feet slapping. Her
water pan was empty and her bill was all gummed up
with mud from rooting around under the bushes. I
turned on the hose and ran water into the old blue-
enameled roasting pan, which has always seemed to me
a sinister sort of water dish for a duck, but really
shouldn't by now since it's obvious that nobody will
ever eat Donald. It was obvious a year ago last fall
when she laid her first egg.

I looked through the fence at the daffodils in the
yard next door. (Donald ate all of ours.) Then I watched
the water swirl and sparkle, listening to it splash and
to the funny flibbling noise Donald makes when she
drinks, and thought about Joe St. George.

His death did not surprise me. Joe was a paraplegic,
paralysed from the waist down, and I knew that there
were still a quantity of metal fragments inside him that
they couldn't take out for one reason and another, each
piece ready to kill him at almost any time. If I was surprised at all, it was only at the fact that he lasted as
long as he did.

That was an odd and horrid thing to put down. Was
I glad to have him dead? Glad for him because I knew
how much pain he'd been in so much of the time, or
glad for me because I felt it was about time I was let
off the hook? Was I relieved or sorry? Or maybe mad
at him for doing it? I just plain didn't know.

I turned off the water, left Donald sitting in it, and
went around the corner of the garage. It's a double,
heated garage and Brock keeps his mice there. As soon
as I opened the door the musty, musky small-mammal-
house zoo-smell of a lot of mice hit me. I took a deep

6

breath because I've discovered from long experience that that's the quickest way to get used to it. I have nothing against mice, I can take them or leave them, but I do wish they didn't smell so.

Brock was sitting on a high lab stool by the workbench under the window petting a mouse. It was a very young one, but big enough to have hair and its eyes were just open. At that age baby mice are so fat they look more like miniaturized pigs than anything, and they are very soft and velvety. In the corner where Brock keeps the individual cages with mother mice, a black mouse was busy paper hanging, as Brock calls it. She was so pregnant she looked like a bug-eyed golfball with a tail. When mice make nests they are incredibly busy, like neurotic housewives. They pick up enormous (for them) pieces of newspaper and put them up against the opening of the nest box and pat them with their front paws, like frantic paper hangers without paste. They bustle around and pause to cut up the paper with a sound like a miniature typewriter. They stuff paper in and pull it back out again, and rearrange it. I never get tired of watching them. I went over to watch this one. "You forgot to give Donald her water," I said almost automatically."

"She's your duck too."

"You were out first." Sometimes I wonder why we talk to each other; I know what Brock's going to say ahead of time, and I bet he knows what I'm going to say; we always say the same things. Watching Mrs. Mouse pause, then gobble up some birdseed, cracking the shells, eating the kernels, picking up the next seed in her paws, I thought about that and wondered when it was that my brother and I had become so strange to

each other. It had happened so imperceptibly that nobody had noticed, and we still bickered in the same old
way, so on the surface of things it looked the same as
ever. Brock's only fifteen months older than I am and
there was a time when we were close as twins. Perhaps
what happened five years ago was what started the
change. We had a guilty secret cementing us together
in a conspiracy of silence, but that same secret made it
difficult for us to be natural together, to talk of inconsequential things. I don't mean that we didn't talk about
inconsequential things, what I mean is that we were
so often thinking about something else that the every-
day sort of responses to each other became formalized
and abstracted so we spoke automatically without really
paying attention.

Like a liturgy. There's meaning there, but the phrases
become so familiar that they lose their meaning, and
just sort of flow along the channels already worn for
them. So instead of saying what you mean, you talk in
order to avoid thinking, even sometimes talk to avoid
thinking about what you're saying.

The way I put that down it looks as if I'd thought of
it myself, but really, it was my mother. She wrote a
poem, she's something of a poet, and Dad says if she'd
send her stuff out she'd be published, but she doesn't
so she isn't.

Mom's something of an odd-ball, a kook. I guess one
word for it might be eccentric. For one thing she's
almost the only person I know who really believes and
acts on "Thou shalt love thy neighbor." She's an Episcopalian and if you consider going to church Sundays and
Holy days devout, I guess you might call her devout.
On the other hand she's not what you generally think

8

of as reverent, and she's not a bit pious . . . if anything she's the opposite. She's always shocking the Episcopal rector, Mr. Cartwright; in fact she was slightly excommunicated once for something she said and had to take it back later. And things strike her funny . . . the kinds of things that really are funny but nobody else dares laugh at. Like the time Mr. Cartwright was preaching on the impermanence of earthly possessions and whammed his fist down on the rail of the pulpit and the whole thing fell off in a cloud of termite-dust.

Just to fill in a little more, Dad's an atheist but the kind that doesn't have to run around trying to convert people, so he and Mom get along just fine and even talk about religion without arguing. Brock's a mystic at the moment, on a sort of semi-Hindu kick. I don't know where I stand. Sometimes I go to church with Mom, and I've been confirmed so I'm officially Episcopal, but mostly religion isn't something I think about one way or the other. Neither Brock nor I ever went to Sunday school. Dad never minded us going to church, but he objects to Sunday school on the grounds that religion, like liquor, is not for children. Mom says that he has a point, considering the brand of religion generally dispensed in Sunday school, and also said that she'd just as soon leave us home Sundays because we don't get to see much of our father during the week. Mom also said that when she was a kid she hated Sunday school and spent most of it hiding in a coal-bin with the boys, giggling. It was so dirty in there that they couldn't sit down or even touch the walls, but they'd stand there in the dark and giggle rather than go to class.

9

But I've gotten off what I was talking about. I asked Brock, "Did you see in the paper about Joe St. George?"

"Yes, the obit was all over the front page. All that slop about how the town will miss him made me mad. None of them ever spoke to him except Mrs. Root and she didn't like him."

"I didn't read it, just got the news he was dead from Mom."

"Now he's dead everybody loved him like mad and he was everybody's bosom buddy. It makes me sick. What did Mom say?"

"Nothing about that part of it. She just told me he'd died and mentioned the list of decorations." Mrs. Mouse disappeared behind her construction of newspaper and didn't seem about to come out again so I turned back to Brock. "She said, 'May God have mercy on his soul.' At first I thought she was kidding, but she wasn't. Do you suppose she knows?"

Brock had picked up some more young mice and they were milling around, crawling up his arms. Half a dozen had gone to sleep in an uneasy heap in the hollow of his palm. "I don't think so," he said after some deliberation. "I wonder if perhaps she suspects now, but back when it happened I don't think she knew."

"That would explain why she's never said anything. If she didn't suspect at first she wouldn't have said anything of course, and later on she probably wasn't sure and even if she had been, what's the use in raking up old bones?"

"There are times when I wish Mom wasn't such a kook," Brock said. "You never can figure her out."

There wasn't much I could say to that. It got very quiet in the garage. Outside Donald was walking around quacking in that bored, lazy-sounding way ducks do when they want to hear themselves talk. I could hear some young mice squeaking inside one of the nest boxes, the snipping of mice teeth as they cracked sunflower seeds. Brock has about three hundred mice in five kinds of cages. He has a big cage of males, a big cage of females, a cage with young mice in it, and a bunch of nest cages for mother mice. He raises a strain of white and a strain of black mice and sells them to a lab inland that uses them to test drugs and things. He sends one hundred a month every month and he's saving the money towards medical school. Dad and Mom are sending us to college but after that it'll be up to us. Brock's eighteen and this year he starts; I go next year, I'm seventeen.

Brock poured his double handful of young mice back into their cage and went to wash his hands. "The trouble is," he said, "now Joe's dead I don't know what to think."

"About what?"

"About what happened, about Joe himself. Everything."

"Me neither. I can't even decide how I feel about him being dead, glad or sad or what."

Brock wiped his hands with unusual care and came back to sit on his stool. "I think I'm relieved," he said after a while. "It solves the problem. I mean, it doesn't matter any more if we tell or not."

"We swore a dreadful swear not to ever tell," I reminded him.

"Don't be childish, Jessica."

"All right." I agreed. I knew that the promise not to tell was intended only to protect Joe; I'd only reminded

Brock to tease him. "It's been so long now it hardly seems worth telling," I said. "Besides, by now it's so complicated it'd take two days just to explain how, why, and wherefore."

"What do you mean?"

"To explain why we didn't tell at the time."

Brock scratched his head. "Stop to think of it, I don't know why we didn't. We just didn't."

"We must have had a reason."

"What was it then, Smartypants?"

"*I* don't know, but that doesn't mean there wasn't one."

"Oh shut up, you sound like Mom."

I almost said "Thank you," but that always makes Brock mad and I didn't want to start a fight. Instead I asked, "But anyway, you wouldn't care if I told now, right?" I was beginning to get an idea.

"No, why should I? Joe's dead, nobody can do anything to him any more. Besides, it was you who really decided not to tell."

"Would you mind making it official?"

"What do you mean official?" Brock was looking at me as if I'd sprouted antlers.

"Don't tell me you've forgotten that paper we buried!"

"Paper?" He paused and looked at the ceiling with his mouth ajar. "Oh. Paper, yes . . . under the tool shed. I remember now." Then he sat up straight, his eyes bright, suddenly all full of interest, "Hey, maybe we put down why we weren't telling. Didn't we put down everything? Which is why we had such an awful time figuring out a safe place to hide it."

"You're right," I agreed, all full of enthusiasm too.

Brock took down a trowel from the tool rack and we went out and around the tool shed to the back corner behind the lilac bushes. The bushes were just coming into leaf and were wet from last night's rain. I held my skirts tight around my legs and let Brock do the digging. Donald came up to investigate, as she always does, and when Brock dug up a worm she began getting in his way, sticking her head into the hole looking for more. I thought I was going to have to hold her, but even with her help, it only took Brock a minute to turn up the bottle we'd put the paper in. It was an old whisky bottle with a screw top.

At the time we'd buried it, we'd dug a deep, deep hole, or so it seemed then. I guess a deep hole when you're eleven isn't so deep any more when you're seventeen. We left Donald eating earthworms and took the bottle into the garage.

Brock washed the mud off and worked at the cap. It was pretty tight, but it came off just when Brock was about to resort to a wrench. The paper inside was a little damp and smelled mildewy but we could read it easily enough. It was written in pencil on sheets of Dad's billing paper. "I sure had lousy handwriting back then," Brock said, spreading the sheets of paper out on the workbench.

Our memories had played us another trick; what had seemed a very long and complete document turned out to be a few words scrawled in very large handwriting. There were four sheets of paper but Brock had written so big that a couple of sentences filled them up and ran over onto the backs.

It said: "Brock John Brewer and Jessica Ruth Brewer hereby state that we saw it happen. We hereby state that we won't ever, never tell, not ever, anybody, or Else, so help us God." It had been signed in red ink with our full names. The ink had run all over, dyeing the paper pink, but you could still read the signatures. My handwriting had been even worse than Brock's.

Brock read it, then I read it, then we looked at each other. Brock said, "At least we knew our own names," and we began to laugh.

So much for documents from the past illuminating everything. I'd thought we'd put down everything, down to the last most insignificant detail. I said so to Brock.

"Me too," he said. "Remember how we looked for a hiding place because we were so sure we'd set down all kinds of incriminating information? Boy, oh boy!"

"Every word 'spoke volumes' as they say in the pulps."

"Maybe so, but they're not talking now." Brock picked up the soggy papers, wadded them up, and dropped them into the trash can in the corner. "O.K.," he said, "for what it's worth, that's formally disposed of." He was looking at me curiously.

"Thanks," I said, not satisfying his curiosity. I'd been slowly growing the idea of trying to write everything down, to try and remember all about Joe St. George and what happened and why we didn't tell. But I wasn't that sure I was going to at that moment, and I wasn't about to stick my neck out for Brock to laugh my head off.

The more I thought about it though, afterwards, the more it seemed to me that I'd never been able to forget Joe (I don't mean forget Joe-the-person, I mean forget what he did and all) or be just a simple, happy kid

14

again unless I got rid of the secret. Maybe it's too late for that by now even if I do tell about it, but even so I would like to try to get rid of it, because it *has* been a burden, a real drag.

So I'm writing it all down, starting at the beginning, which is the only way it makes sense to do it. I'm going to have to reconstruct as well as just remember, so I'll have to put down everything that seems to me to go with the story. Mom says "The truth shall set you free." Well, I'm going to give it the old try and just see.

2

I suppose there are hundreds of places that could properly be called the beginning: Joe St. George was born and grew up in San Francisco, and who knows what things happened when he was a kid that made him grow up one way and not another? But he never talked about being a kid, and I can't imagine him a day younger than he was when I met him. Another starting place might be when he was in the war, or when he was wounded, or when he discovered he'd never walk again. I know he enlisted in the Army at the beginning of World War II and that he'd been a professional soldier, but he didn't talk about that. He was wounded in 1951 and spent the next six years being put back together in Army hospitals, first in Japan, then in the States, but he never talked about that either. He talked so little about himself that I didn't even know he'd been on Omaha Beach until I read it in the paper.

So I guess the only thing for me to do is to start

where it started for me. With the old Prescott place, and with the name: St. George.

The old Prescott place is an old, old house on a small rise of ground just to the lee of the breakwater on the right shore of the harbor, facing out. It's a small house, an architectural oddity, and to judge by the number of summer people who take snapshots and paint water-colors of it, downright picturesque. It has clapboard walls and scrollwork carving tucked away in odd corners, and the ridgepole has a slight convex curve. The shipwrights who made wooden ships used to build houses like that, with the ribs supporting the roof and the ridgepole curved slightly . . . as if the builder couldn't get the shape of a keel out of his mind's eye and had to make houses that would, if turned wrong-side up, prove seaworthy. The whole house is con-structed with the kind of care that used to go into making old sailing ships; it was made of seasoned wood and put together with treenails, so although it was abandoned for decades it has remained sound. It has weathered to the silver-gray color of old driftwood and there's a very slight leeward list to it, as if it had had to give just a little before the winter gales that blow in off the North Atlantic. There is a small sand yard with a few patches of tough wiry grass here and there, sur-rounded by a dilapidated split-rail fence except on the side bordering the water. Along the fence there is a jungle of huge elderberry bushes, some wild roses, a lot of tall woody-stemmed weeds, and a sprinkling of poison ivy.

Before Joe St. George bought it, the old Prescott place was empty and had been empty for a couple of generations. I think it was owned by the Prescott estate, at any rate it was tied up in some kind of legal red tape.

At one time there were a lot of Prescotts around Mackerel Cove; in fact, there's a Prescott Road on the other side of the salt marsh. But there aren't any around now and haven't been for years and years. We kids all knew why the Prescotts all moved away; it's the kind of story kids know and adults (who talk about it in front of kids) are always surprised to find out they know. The reason they moved away was that Mr. Elijah Prescott came back from the Civil War and led a lynching party. Afterwards it was discovered that the man they'd hanged wasn't guilty. Guilty of what? Nobody seems to know; the reason for hanging anyone at all seems to have been totally forgotten.

With this suitably gruesome background and an abandoned house to go with it, we naturally decided that the house had to be haunted. Supposedly by the man who'd been hanged by mistake. There's nothing like the memory of an old, uncorrectable wrong to give a place a reputation for evil. We kids habitually used the yard as part of a shortcut (it really should be called a longcut, it was at least twice as far as going by the road) to town and we'd discovered the rotting stump of a tree. Naturally we arrived at the conclusion that the hanging in question had occurred in that exact spot, and that the Prescotts had cut down the tree before leaving town. We were unmoved by the information, given us by our parents, that the tree in question had fallen of its own accord the year before the breakwater was built, and that the lynching had taken place somewhere else entirely.

The year I was nine and Brock was ten we and

Bobby Wyddyn and Oakley Malone worked up the nerve to break into the house. It was a broiling hot day, a real brain-frier, with a gusty wind that blew sand up to sting our legs at the beach, which is why we thought up something else to do. Oakley had a big fat candle and Brock had a box of wooden kitchen matches. We softened the leading around one of the panes in the window by the front door and finally were able to work the pane out. We hadn't the nerve to break a window. We reached in and unlocked the front door from the inside and discovered that it was a Dutch door and the bottom half required a key. The top half had an old-fashioned bolt so we could get that open easily enough, but when we discovered how difficult it was to climb over the bottom half we very nearly called the whole thing off. We wanted a quicker exit in case of spooks.

I gathered a handful of elderberries and sat in the shade of the bushes eating them while the boys argued. I remember being glad I was a girl so I didn't have to always run around proving I was really a man the way boys do.

Oakley used to be a skinny little kid, real small and stringy. He was so blonde he was nearly albino and he always had little strips of sunburned skin hanging off the end of his nose. Aside from the places he got sunburned he was very pale, and with the enormous white front teeth he had and his queer violet eyes he looked like a white rabbit more than anything else. His mother always made him wear a big farmer-type straw hat and the one he had on that day had a hole in the brim so a spot of sun kept sliding back and forth across his eyes making him blink. Incidentally, now Oakley's grown up to fit his teeth and he's developed a chin. He's not half bad; in fact, I've heard girls say his violet eyes are sexy. He also uses those new suntan lotions and instead of burning turns a sort of jaundice-yellow that's considerably more attractive than a peeling burn.

Bobby Wyddyn is and was one of those compact, beautifully put-together boys who are the envy of ones like Brock who are long and gangly. Bobby had a brown crew-cut that year and a round, cheerful face like a well-fed cherub. He hasn't changed much except that he isn't as chubby now. Back then he usually had a finger in his nose. That day he was digging away like mad because he was nervous. He extracted a large goober from his left nostril, inspected it, and solemnly as a judge, ate it, nibbling it up with his front teeth. He's outgrown that now, thank goodness.

Brock, as long as I'm describing people, was about two inches taller than anybody. He always had been up until last year when Oakley suddenly grew six inches in six months. Both Brock and I have hazel eyes and red-brown hair . . . well, to be absolutely honest, it's brown with reddish highlights in the sun. Brock had long hair that year; he was afraid of the barber, and the back of his hair hung over his collar about an inch and a half. That year I was wearing pigtails and they were down below my shoulder blades.

Anyway, the boys argued until they ended up double-dast-daring each other right into the house. I went along because, even if I am a girl, I couldn't let them think I was *that* scared. Besides I was curious and it would have been too boring to have waited outside. In any case, nobody expected me to go first.

The house was a let-down after all we'd expected. No bloodstains or guilty confessions or sinister lengths of rope. Nothing at all in fact but little ridges of fine wind-blown sand on the floors, spiders in the corners, and fat green bluebottle flies humming in the bars of dusty sunshine coming through the cracks in the battens protecting the windows. The place smelled faintly of mice (which I found downright homey since Brock had acquired his first pair the year before) and also had a salt, seaweedy odor, like an abandoned shack on a dock. You could hear the waves on the breakwater outside, the bell buoy off the point, and the house seemed to echo faintly to the larger waves. It is very near the water's edge; a lot of land eroded away between the time it was built and 1938 when the breakwater was built, so there's about three yards between the nearest corner of the house and the high-tide mark, with just a steep little beach at the edge of the yard.

We went through the whole place with a fine-tooth comb. There were two rooms upstairs with windows on the ends of the house and sloping ceilings; downstairs there were four rooms, two large and two smallish. One room had smoke stains on the ceiling so we guessed it must have been the kitchen, but there was no bathroom, there were no light fixtures. There wasn't so much as a broken chair or a coathanger or a scrap of old newspaper. We didn't want to be disappointed so we searched every cranny and even looked up the fireplace chimneys hoping for something worth thinking about. Then Bobby found the cellar door and we went down the stairs. Oakley went first holding what was left of the candle. The cellar was damp and smelled moldy, and just going down from the heat of the closed-up house into the damp, cool dark, we all began to get goosebumps. It was black as the inside of your head down there and we couldn't see a thing outside the little sphere of light thrown by Oakley's candle stump. We therefore imagined the darkness into the shape of every dank, dreary, dreadful dungeon we'd ever read about.

The steps and floor were stone and as we descended they became distinctly colder under our bare feet and began to feel wet. I think we were all of us set to cut and run from the moment our cringing toes touched the floor and found it slimy. Then Oakley yelped and dropped the candle and we all took off like scalded cats for the great outdoors. We just about flew over the bottom half of that door and didn't stop running until we got to the Coastguard Station. There, under the protection of the Almighty and the U.S. Coastguard (though we saw neither hide nor hair of either) we sat down on the brick wall around the grounds of the Station and collected ourselves. Oakley said he'd seen Something. His description started out very vague but it improved as he went along until he ended up with an evocation of a hanged man that stood our hair on end. I can still remember him standing there with his head lolling loosely on his shoulder and his tongue hanging out the corner of his mouth.

Much later Oakley confided to me that he'd actually stepped on something squishy and made up the ghost afterwards to avoid being teased for being the first one to start running. He said that by the time he'd finished telling the story he'd more than half-believed it himself. I'd had a doozy of a nightmare about Oakley's ghost but I didn't hold it against him. After all, the expedition would have been a total failure if it hadn't been for him.

In the middle of the afternoon we all crept back together and shut the top half of the door, relocked it, and stuck the pane of glass back in with some electrician's tape Bobby borrowed from his father's tool chest. Respect for property had nothing to do with it; we didn't want the ghost getting out that night. We were still scared half to death and Oakley and Bobby had brought their Holy Medals for protection. Brock and I had to make do with a clove of garlic borrowed from the kitchen and Mom's plain silver cross she wears Sundays. Brock had been reading vampire and werewolf stories and he said that silver and garlic ought to work for ghosts too. I wasn't so sure. I remember feeling bitter because Dad had said Holy Medals were pure superstition and Mom agreed and wouldn't let me have one.

Anyway, for a while after that we avoided the house and property, but it was inconvenient because, as I said, it was right in the middle of one of our favourite routes into the village; so it wasn't long before we were cutting through same as always. We continued avoiding the house itself though. We knew there was nothing interesting in it with the exception of a possible ghost, which was too frightening to be any fun.

That winter the house went on the market, something about the estate being settled after some kind of long-drawn-out litigation. A few batches of people turned up towards spring to look at it, but Mr. O'Connor, the real estate man, said it was going to be hard to sell because there was no plumbing or electricity. Then we heard that somebody had bought it, and next it was wired and plumbing was installed. We were still in school though, so we didn't get to see much of the work being done. Then one afternoon a moving van passed the school and we heard that furniture and things had been moved into the house. But by the time we got out of school the stuff had all been moved and the van was gone. The windows were still boarded up so we couldn't see in, though we tried. We even discussed trying to take out the pane of glass (which had been fixed) again, but decided not to. Now that somebody clearly owned the house we knew we had no business breaking in.

Then nothing happened for quite a while. For about a week we kept close tabs on the house, waiting to see who was going to live there, but when nobody came we forgot about it again. The weather was pretty crummy too that month, which discouraged us from hanging around anyplace outside.

Then one raw, rainy day I decided to go up to Dad's office instead of walking across the cold windy causeway. He generally has short hours Wednesday and Friday in the off-season, so there was a good chance of getting a ride home in half an hour or so. It was near the beginning of the month and he had some magazines I hadn't seen so I curled up in the corner of the only really comfortable chair in the waiting room (which was otherwise empty, a good sign) and began reading.

I was just getting interested in a story when Mrs. Root sailed in. I scrunched down small so she wouldn't notice me, and she went on past into Dad's office. I heard her telling Dad that she'd dropped her bridge and bent it.

Mrs. Root owns the Lobster Pot Gift Shoppe, which is on the sea side of Main Street between it and the seawall. She is a widow and she looks like a wicked queen. She has glossy black hair and big, rather dull, black eyes which she makes up with fancy eyeshadows, the color depending on the current style. She has long, slender hands and she wears her fingernails very long. They're those convex talon-like nails that you see on the hands used to advertise handcream on TV so I suppose somebody must find them attractive. She uses whatever the fashionable shade of nailpolish is and I've never seen it chipped. She takes good care of her hands and seems very fond of them, for she is always displaying them in dramatic poses.

Dad jokingly calls her the Mackerel Cove Clarion because she always scoops the *Defender* when it comes to news. If you want the current low-down you don't read the paper, you go to see Mrs. Root at the Lobster Pot. People with news go there too; it's a village habit, which is odd, stop to think of it, because nobody likes Mrs. Root very much.

This time, without Dad's fingers in her mouth, she was going great guns while he fixed her bridge. She has a carrying voice but I wasn't listening, in fact I was trying to ignore her. But when I heard her mention the old Prescott place she had my undivided attention.

She said that Mr. St. George had moved in a week before, that he was a cripple in a wheelchair and that he put ships into bottles for a hobby. She said he had a total disability pension from the Government and, as I recall, knew how much he was getting a month down to the last cent. She had a good deal to say about the bottled ships and I got the distinct impression that she was very impressed with them. She always runs down anything she buys when she's talking to villagers for fear that somebody will find out what something is worth. When she's trying to sell something to a summer person it's another story entirely. Then all of a sudden it metamorphoses into a Priceless Antique or a Unique Work of Art. It's really awful how she lies. Mom, who's too darn tolerant sometimes, says Mrs. Root is acquisitive. Everybody else says she's a miser. I know one thing, she doesn't pay her dental bills. She owes Dad $600 for past work and a new upper plate. She still owes for work done on the teeth that had to be pulled when she got the plate.

We kids used to sell her stuff we picked up off the rocks and beach. Things like those round fishnet corks with a hole in the middle, fancy-looking driftwood, lobster floats whose owners we didn't know (if we knew who owned a float we always returned it), and the very small crab and snail shells that you find in straw washed up high into the saltgrass in the marsh. She embeds the shells in plastic and sells them for paperweights, and she takes the corks, puts a ten-cent candle in them, dribbles wax around and sells them for $2.50. She paid us a nickel a cork. About the time we were ten we decided she was underpaying us and went on strike, but the next thing we knew a bunch of little kids had showed up and were willing to beachcomb at her prices, so that was the end of that.

Anyway, it was from overhearing Mrs. Root that I first heard about Joe St. George. After she got through talking about the bottled ships she went on to describe him. She said he was horribly disfigured, that half his face was a mass of scars, so from that side he looked like a gargoyle. She had endless reservations about the wisdom of a person who was confined to a wheelchair living all alone in the Prescott place, and she went on and on about that. She said she'd talked to the "young man" (this phrase didn't convey any information because she used it in reference to any male from the age of ten to seventy), and she'd told him for his own-good-of-course how foolish he was being. Apparently he had not taken this advice kindly and had been rude to her and she was of the opinion that he was an ungrateful clod, or words to that effect.

The fact that Mrs. Root disliked Joe St. George amounted to a sterling character reference as far as I was concerned. The only person in town she's remained on consistent speaking terms with is Mr. Felcon who is a pruney little Protestant minister who runs a vaguely interfaith Protestant church that is mostly attended by summer people and a small group of middle-aged gossips. Mr. Felcon's church is a graceful white clapboard structure with a steeple copied after one of the more famous Colonial churches in Salem or Boston or someplace like that. It used to be Congregational but now it's sort of nothing in particular, sort of semi-Baptist-Methodist with free-form prayers and stuff like that. I've never been in it but I've looked in the door and they have red plush padding on the seats and no place to kneel. No altar either, just a dining table and an enormous pulpit.

More than half the people here belong to the Church of the Immaculate Conception, which is an immense red brick affair all set about with twelve-foot concrete saints and angels. It's across from the school, and is a shining example to why this recent movement to combine different churches won't work. There used to be a French church and an Irish church in town, but the big wheels decided that it would be better to have just one good big church instead of two little broken-down ones, so when they built this new one they combined the two. There's a French priest and an Irish priest and as far as I know they've never been on speaking terms. The Irish priest annoys the French priest by being very informal and down-to-earth. The French priest infuriates the Irish priest by sailing around town dressed in a cassock and biretta and looking ethereal and fasting very ostentatiously. They take every other service, and the French half of the congregation goes to the French priest's services and the Irish half to the Irish priest's and never the twain shall meet, except by accident in the parking lot. And you'd be surprised how many lawsuits have started in the parking lot. A couple of times a year a Monseigneur or Bishop or something shows up and begs (twice so as to get the message to both halves of the congregation) for tolerance, with no noticeable effect. I've been to the church a couple of times with Oakley who belongs to the Irish half or Bobby who belongs to the French half (the division is not strictly along national lines) and I kind of like the candles and things.

The only other church in town is St. Jude's, the Episcopal church. It's a moth-eaten little stone building which looks sort of abandoned because half the tower has slumped and kind of fallen in. It's old as all get-out, and it's all the way around the other side of the harbor, near the cemetery. In summer it's like a tomb and so damp you have to take a sweater with you. You keep expecting dew to collect on you as you sit. It smells strongly of seaweed, I don't know why, it isn't that near the water. In winter it has drafts like no drafts you've ever felt; you could practically fly a kite on them, and if you drop a piece of paper it takes off down the aisle.

In fall and spring it's not so bad. I go with Mom some-times, mostly to make her feel good; not that she says anything, but I can tell. I don't much go for the rector, Mr. Cartwright. He's one of those cold, severe types and looks as if he was made of something more like wood than meat; he's square and broad but neither fat nor muscular. He usually has a faintly pained look on his face, as if his hair shirt itches but he's too well-mannered to scratch. I think I recall Doc Elsinger say-ing once he has rheumatism, which figures. I guess he's Godly as all get-out, but he's the kind of person you'd rather die than tell a problem to. He and the Irish priest are buddies.

But back to Mr. Felcon. Mr. Felcon is one of those sickly-sweet people, much given to dispensing the kind of platitude that sticks to your teeth. He and Mrs. Root are usually thick as thieves; they spend hours standing side-by-side looking out of Mrs. Root's store window at the main street with a disapproving air. Mr. Felcon ex-pands like a banty rooster on these occasions and you can see him talking away a mile a minute, with Mrs. Root listening attentively with a slightly sheep-like expression on her face that doesn't fit at all with her wicked-queen make-up. Mr. Felcon has a wife, but she's so unassuming as to be practically non-existent. She's one of those pale, gray, monotone people who sort of float around in the corners of things like shadows. If she were a little more real I'd feel sorry for her, but I simply can't bring myself to believe in her existence (like a sort of half-gone ghost).

As I said, Mr. Felcon and Mrs. Root are buddies, and half the town says they have some sort of vaguely hopeless passion for each other. The idea is disgusting to me, like imagining a frog in love with an armadillo. Mr. Felcon is about five feet three and Mrs. Root is six feet even. Mr. Felcon is weedy, like a stereotype of a pickpocket, pointy nose and furtive walk and all, and Mrs. Root is built like an Amazon. It's true that nobody likes Mrs. Root but I still can't see what makes her listen to Mr. Felcon.

Mr. Felcon has his small circle of admirers, mostly middle-aged women who are widows or else don't get on with their husbands. They sort of follow in his wake and quote him when they talk, and in general are pretty disgusting. All of them gossip like mad and spend half their time in Mr. St. Laurent's drug store doing it over cups of tea and the kind of sticky bakery goods that overweight people like to eat. They're not all fat; the worst one is thin as a broom and eats like a shrew.

Mom says I shouldn't be intolerant. All right. The reason Mr. Felcon walks furtively, like an amateur shoplifter expecting to be caught, is Adonis. Adonis is a very large white collie with a lame hind leg that belongs to Antoine O'Brien the sailmaker. Adonis has a perverse, unseemly and totally incomprehensible passion for Mr. Felcon. Every time Adonis sees him he comes up behind him and gives him a big selfish goose with his nose, and once or twice he has knocked him down and tried to mount him. It's all very hopeless from everybody's point of view, Adonis's as well as Mr. Felcon's. The result of being sneaked up on all the time is that Mr. Felcon has a habit of looking nervously over his shoulder as he walks, and of backing up to a wall when he stops to talk to someone outdoors. I can see how it must be unnerving to be sneaked up on by a very large dog and goosed every time you relax your guard, especially if you've got no sense of humor at all. Mr Felcon has never, to my knowledge, admitted that Adonis exists, which takes some doing, considering.

Personally, I like Adonis much better than I like Mr. Felcon. He doesn't do it to anyone else, and altogether he's a fine upstanding citizen. He even saved one of the O'Brien kids from drowning three years ago. I don't recall which one, there are a dozen and a half of them, but it was one of the smaller ones. It fell off Mr. O'Brien's wharf and Adonis barked until help came. Adonis is a really fine dog; he's gentle with children, he doesn't chase cats, and he guards Mr. O'Brien's wharf at night.

The day I first heard about Joe St. George, Mrs. Root said also that Mr. Felcon planned to call on him and invite him to join "Community Activities" which means go to Mr. Felcon's church services. She said the "poor boy" ought to be helped to feel welcome, to "be-long." Which is, I suppose, a commendable enough sentiment and no doubt genuine since it didn't earn her any money. Then Mrs. Root started to tell Dad how to run his office so I unfolded myself and quietly stole away. When Dad's had a how-to-do-it session with Mrs. Root he's not fit company for anyone, and I pre-ferred to walk home in the rain. I also wanted to get out of there before she came out into the waiting room and started in on me.

Mr. Felcon didn't get to see Joe St. George for a month though. Around the beginning of spring Mr. Felcon always begins to get a haunted look around the eyes, like the man in the Before picture of a laxative advertisement. Then the next thing you know he takes to bed with hives and stays there, ministered to by his wife but otherwise incommunicado, for about a month. He calls it "Rose fever." I don't know why, since there aren't any roses out that time of year, and anyway I didn't know rose fever had anything to do with hives. I suppose it figures that a guy like him would be allergic to spring. But Mom says I shouldn't be intolerant.

What I meant to get to was to say that I know how Joe acted before he met Mr. Felcon, because I met Joe the following day.

3

There's a book in the library with a big colored picture of St. George and the Dragon. It shows a pallid
young man with a supercilious smirk on his face (which
is the only part of him not totally encased in very
durable-looking armor) spearing a very small dragon
with a very long spear. St. G. is sitting way up on top
of a big fat horse and the dragon has a sad soulful
expression. It's a picture guaranteed to make you feel
sorry for the dragon. I saw the picture long before I
heard about Joe St. George. I'd gone down to the library
on a long, dull winter afternoon to get out some new
books and return the ones I had. At the time I was
methodically reading my way through all the animal
books in the place, alphabetically, but Brock, as always,
had an awful time deciding what he wanted. While I
was waiting for Brock to make up his mind I saw this
big art book on the table and stopped to page through it.

The St. G. picture caught my attention partly because

there were animals in it, partly because it was so realistically done and I was trying to figure out how the artist managed to make the armor look so hard and metallic, and partly because I was puzzled. I couldn't see what was so big about going out all done up in iron plate to stick a little old lizard. I read the text (skipping the part about the artist) and it described a real monster of a dragon and made an epic battle out of the lizard-sticking. I couldn't figure out what the artist had had against St. G. to make him look like such a dope. The dragon in the picture wasn't big or fierce enough to catch chickens, much less run around terrorizing and laying waste a countryside and eating fair young maidens and things like that. (Why were dragons always supposed to eat slender, fair young maidens? Why not big, fat juicy tender ones? That's what I'd eat if I were a dragon.)

Anyway, the name St. George meant dragons to me, big vigorous ones. There was a time when I believed in dragons. The year I met Joe St. George I was just on the edge of belief. I knew perfectly well, if anyone had asked me, that dragons don't exist, but I still hoped they did. Once Mom quoted me something about being the kind of person who would do anything to see a unicorn, even a dead one. That's me.

So. St. George was a name full of magic and all kinds of romantic connotations. Of course I knew perfectly well that even if somebody named St. George had killed a dragon that this one was probably no relation. I also knew that the dragon-slaying St. G. was long since dead and moldered into dust. (Passage of time wasn't my strong point at that age, but I wasn't stupid.) The point is that I wanted very much to believe that this was the one and only St. George, so I did. Just like that. And at that age it wasn't hard at all. Mrs. Root's description of him only made me more sure because, after all, it would be a pretty poor sort of dragon that wouldn't fight back.

As I walked home that afternoon with dragons in my head I made up my mind to visit Mr. St. George (weather permitting) the following morning. The fact he was living in the old Prescott place also proved him a genuine hero, for who else would dare dispossess the uneasy ghost of a wronged man?

Before I ever met Joe I had constructed a fact-proof suspension of disbelief, and for me he was always something special, more than human. That's one reason it's so difficult for me to remember him accurately. I never wanted to see him as he was but as I wished he was. I made allowances for him and overlooked things he did in order to preserve my image of him. All the way along it was a case of, "My mind's made up, don't confuse me with the facts."

By the time I got home that afternoon I was wet as a fish from the wind blowing rain up inside my slicker and down my neck. It was altogether shaping up into a wild night. The gulls were flying inland, crying bitterly to each other as they went, there were whitecaps on the water and I could hear the bell buoy ringing like crazy. I looked back toward the village and saw that old Captain O'Brien, who is the local weather prophet, had run up the two triangular pennants that mean a gale warning. (One triangular is small-craft warning, two a gale; one square is full gale and two square is hurricane.) As usual the Captain was right, and the weatherman didn't predict a gale until the six o'clock report on the radio. By bedtime the wind had risen to somewhere around thirty-five knots. I wished the weather would

35

come and go before morning but I had little hope of it. I not only was dying to visit St. George, but the prospect of a Saturday indoors didn't appeal to me.

As it turned out, the storm blew itself out before morning leaving behind a crisp wind and heavy seas to show it had been there. I gobbled my breakfast and was off in the early sunshine. Everything was drenched and had that bright brand-new look that follows a storm. There were specks of rainbow caught in left-over raindrops and the grass by the road was full of sparkling fairy handkerchiefs (which were really cobwebs). The gulls were wheeling overhead complaining rustily. I remember skipping along the bumpy asphalt road singing something loud and happy because I felt so good. Everything, it seemed, showed good omens. (I was very omen-conscious in those days.)

Before I could see it I heard the surf booming on the breakwater, a different more sinister note than the usual sound of surf on the shore: I temporarily forgot what I'd come that way for and instead of turning off at the Prescott place I kept going toward the base of the breakwater. The tide was in full flood and monstrous breakers were creaming over all but the highest rocks. The breakwater is made of enormous chunks of rough-cut granite dumped higgledy-piggledy on top of each other. They have sharp edges and corners and there are crevices and empty cave-like spaces all through. The wind keens and wails in the caves and the sea sucks and shouts and giggles and makes strange hollow sounds deep down inside.

I approached from upwind to avoid being wetted down by the spray and stood there watching for quite a long while. The earth under my feet vibrated slightly to the impact of the combers and, without noticing, I just kept edging closer and closer. Even if I'd been noticing I would have had a hard time keeping away from all that lovely violence. This time, before I knew it, there I was out on the breakwater itself right in the middle of all that marvelous tumult and racket. The stone under my feet quivered to the smash of the waves and I felt ten feet tall and invincible.

The next thing I knew a big wave came sloshing over the rock I was standing on and swept my feet out from under me. I went slithering over the sharp edge, scraping my leg from my ankle to the edge of my shorts, and I only just managed to catch hold of a corner with my hands and to brace my feet on the rock below. I clambered up and got off the breakwater in record time. My heart was pounding so hard I could barely catch my breath and I thought it was going to hammer its way right out of my chest.

Standing on dry land I looked back at that white water boiling along the edges of the boulders and got scareder than ever. There is a current there, especially at the beginning of the ebb, that can suck even a good swimmer down and drag him along the rocks at the bottom, around the end of the breakwater and out to sea. It has happened more than once, and if it happens you're not only dead, you're a messy corpse. The bodies turn up approximately one week (depending on the winds) later at Turner's Harbor.

My heart calmed down a little once it got through to me that I hadn't fallen in, and then I realized that my leg hurt, I was cold and wet, and my sneakers were full of water. I was about to start home for comfort and first-aid when I heard someone calling to me. I had the vague feeling that, stop to think of it, he'd been calling for some time, but I hadn't heard.

I took my knuckles out of my eyesockets and turned to look. You can see most of the front yard of the Prescott place from the base of the breakwater, and I saw a man in a wheelchair coming toward the fence. I think I must have stopped crying about then. He stopped when he knew he'd caught my eye and beckoned to me. I limped over, it was only a few steps to the fence, and climbed on through. I remember I'd stopped crying by the time I was through the fence. I would have forgotten to limp if my leg hadn't hurt so awfully. The message that it hurt was still being sent, but I'd stopped paying attention to it, it wasn't registering.

St. George was a big man. At least, his shoulders and chest were big, he had a bullneck and his arms were big around as many men's legs. He had smaller hands than you'd expect from the bulk of the rest of him, but they were actually about average size. He had a deep tan, which looked exotic and surprised me that early in the year, and against it the thick scars on his face and running down his neck to be hidden by his shirt stood out in bold relief. They were the kind of scars called keloid. What happens is, instead of a cut or something healing nice and flat the way you'd expect, the scar tissue keeps growing until there is a big lump of it. Joe's scars were about a quarter of an inch wide and high, like clothes-line cut in half lengthways. His mouth was somewhat distorted by the scarring which netted one side of his face and went up into his hair. One side of his face was almost untouched, the other was ruined. I suppose, objectively, he was a fright, but I thought he was lovely, and I wasn't in the least afraid.

He looked exactly as if he'd been mauled by a dragon, clawed and gnawed at a bit. (I should think a dragon might treat a man the way a cat treats a mouse.) I hadn't learned about keloid scars at the time and I explained them as the effects of dragon-poison.

I must have smiled because he smiled in return. "Hi!" I said enthusiastically, as if I'd been longing to meet him, which I had, or as if he were my long-lost rich uncle. "I bet you're St. George."

"Yes, that's right." He was a trifle confused, which I didn't understand at the time but which I can now see was only natural, considering. After all, he didn't know me from Adam's off ox. But Joe was a man who could think on his feet (figuratively speaking) and he recovered his aplomb quickly. "Call me Joe," he said.

I thought that was remarkably neighborly of him. I was, in fact, downright flattered and slightly overcome. Very few adults would have let me call them by their first names if I'd wanted to (which I didn't) and to be treated like an equal by a genuine hero and dragon-slayer! It was almost too much. I said something earth-shaking like "Gee-whiz," or words to that effect and stood there gawking.

Then Joe pointed to my scrape and said, "Better let me fix that up."

The moment he mentioned it, the message that it hurt suddenly got through again. I looked down, and, forgetting to make allowances for a little blood going a long way especially when mixed with liberal quantities of seawater, I pushed the panic button and began to scream.

Joe took me into the house. He picked me up as if I was a sack of meal and laid me across the arms of the chair, which dug into my back something awful but I didn't dare wriggle for fear of falling. Then he said "Hold on," and wheeled us up the ramp and into the house. Inside he set me on the edge of the kitchen table and set about cleaning my leg. Now that I think back that seems odd. Joe wasn't the kind of person who went around picking people up and taking care of them. He generally went to some trouble to avoid getting his clothes dirty too, and that time I was dripping seawater and blood and messed up his pants for sure. At the time, of course, I didn't think anything of it. I was scared and all I could think about was the places I hurt.

By the time he'd put some sulpha powder on my scrape I'd stopped crying, though my diaphragm was still jerking and there wasn't anything I could do to stop it. I thought the sulpha was a vast improvement on my father's all-purpose cure-all which is iodine. I asked what it was and Joe told me and said it was used in the Service.

I nodded. I already knew from Mrs. Root that he'd been in World War Two and Korea. I knew he'd been wounded in Korea, but I didn't want to discuss it with him because to have done so would have made it more difficult to believe in the dragon. I think that is one of the reasons Joe liked me. I'm probably the only person he ever met who actively did *not* want to know about how he'd been wounded. I know, from the look on his face when Brock asked questions, that he hated to talk about it. It must have been restful for Joe to have one person around who was not bursting with unasked questions. I think it would be more of a strain to be with someone who wanted to ask and didn't than to be with someone who was frankly curious, which is prob-

40

ably one reason he liked Brock and the other kids. Kids don't stare, look away, and speculate the way adults do. If kids are really curious they ask.

I think maybe another reason Joe took to me right off was that I saw him as a whole. Even Brock saw him in terms of good side and bad side and had trouble looking him in the face because he never knew whether to try to avoid looking at the scars or to go ahead and stare. I never had that problem with Joe, probably because he fitted my previously-decided-on mental image so well. I know how Brock felt though. I have that problem with Mr. O'Connor who has a big purple birthmark with hair on it on the side of his neck up to his ear.

Anyway, Joe asked me if I wanted a coke. I wasn't allowed to have coke on account of it being bad for my teeth, so of course I was crazy about it. If he'd offered me champagne I wouldn't have been as pleased; as a matter of fact, at that age I'd probably have been downright displeased. I told him I'd love a coke.

When Joe opened the refrigerator door to get it out I took a good look at what he kept in there. It was crammed wtih coke and canned beer, with one shelf of lunch meat, salami, and things like that. Not a drop of milk-for-the-teeth.

Joe opened the bottle for me and one for himself and handed me the bottle. I thanked him politely (I was a very polite child most of the time). While I drank the coke I told him that when I grew up I was going to have exactly the same things in my refrigerator he had in his, and confided in him that I planned to give *my* children candy with every meal, bubblegum in between, and I was never, never going to make them drink milk.

41

At this he began to laugh. He put back his head and howled. He had a fascinating prosthesis across the roof of his mouth and along the side where the scarring was. It was more than just a bridge and I couldn't tell if it was fixed or some kind of removable plate. It was made mostly of some kind of silver metal. I asked Dad about it and he said he couldn't tell without seeing it, but he'd guess it might be vanadium steel. I never asked Joe about it.

I was hurt and irritated by Joe's laughter. What I'd said wasn't *that* funny, not funny enough to roll in the aisles over. And nobody likes to be laughed at when they're being serious. If Joe had been anybody else I probably would have taken an instant dislike to him and would never have come back. But I made allowances for him because he was a dragon-slayer, and managed to overlook his behaviour.

Incidentally, gratitude had nothing to do with it. Now that I'm seventeen I can see that a total stranger getting slopped up to help a kid they've never seen before is something to be grateful for, but at the age of eleven I assumed adults would take care of me, and simply accepted it as my due. If I said "Thank you," it was merely because I'd been taught to, not because I felt particularly thankful. Like saying "Thank you" to the host or hostess at a birthday party when you've had a terrible time; you say "Thank you" because you know your mother will ask you if you did, and will find out from the kid's mother if you didn't.

Trying to look at it from Joe's point of view I can see that it would be funny to have a skinny little girl with knobby knees, no chest, and wet hair tell you in all seriousnes that she intends to bring up her children a certain way. I suppose the very idea of such a little kid being a mother some day might be funny. But I still say it wasn't that funny.

And even if it was, it would have been kinder not to have laughed so darn hard about it. But then, kindness was not one of Joe St. George's virtues. He seemed to be quite insensitive to other people's feelings, in general. I don't know if he was aware and didn't care or if he didn't know when he was hurting someone in the first place. I can't recall that he ever acted as if he knew; he never apologized.

While I finished up the coke he let me look around the house. Everything was on one floor, obviously, since he had no way of going up stairs. In one room was a hospital bed with pulleys and ropes and things attached to the ceiling, and devices to exercise on, parallel bars and stuff. All that hospital and gym equipment looked terribly exotic in that room with its comfortable Early American proportions and fieldstone fireplace. There was a bathroom with a big tub and more stuff attached to the ceiling. In the living room there was a workbench under the windows overlooking the water. He had all his tools and material for making ships and putting them into bottles there. There was a fine, clean smell of fresh wood chips, glue, and new paint. There were old-fashioned-looking pictures of old sailing ships tacked up on the walls, and a lot of them looked as if they'd been torn out of books and magazines. Later on I found out that he only made models of ships that had actually existed, and did it very accurately too. He also had a viewer for reading microfilm; he was always getting little packets of microfilm from the Library of Congress. There was also a bookcase full of books, mostly on ships.

I remember that once, on a dreary day, when he had just completed a ship and had put the cork in the bottle, Joe said, "There, cork her up, and that's the end of that one." He sounded both gleeful and sad, maybe even a little diabolical. He had a grin on his face that didn't match the expression around his eyes. "See Jessica? I put a whole little crumb of history in this bottle. In there is Blackbeard Teach the pirate, who braided his beard into dozens of little pigtails and went about with lighted slow matches behind his ears. He was one of the most malevolent pirates in history. In that bottle are sea battles and ships sunk with all hands, murder most fell, blood and death. And now I've corked all that up so it'll never get out again. What do you think of that?"

I told him I thought he was teasing, and Joe laughed and said maybe he was at that. Of course he was teasing to some extent, but to what extent was he serious? He never put a ship with a good or noble history into a bottle, only pirate ships and slavers.

Was Joe more like me than I'd ever thought? Were his bottled ships like my dragons? I'm sure he knew that he couldn't really bottle up crumbs of the world's evil by making a model ship and corking it up, but did he hope he could? Or wish he could?

That first visit I was most impressed by two things. One was how much the feeling of the house had changed now that it was wired and piped and so forth and had someone living in it. There was no faintest trace of the former empty feeling, and even in the basement there was no ghostliness. I went down there a couple of times, and it was empty except for a new furnace, a pump, and a couple of lights and it just a stone cellar, that's all. The other thing that impressed me was that the only chair in the entire house was Joe's wheelchair. There was no provision for a guest to sit down.

Later on cushions just sort of appeared here and there, in front of the fireplaces, on the corners of tables, on the left-hand side of the workbench. Joe seemed to prefer us to sit on his unscarred side (though he never made anything out of it) and I, for one, preferred to because it was easier to read his expression on the good side and almost impossible on the other.

The thing I liked best about Joe's house was that everything was down where a kid could reach it. The workbench was low as a dining table, and all the cupboards were low so I could see and reach into all of them. Almost from the beginning Joe gave me the run of the house . . . even the stove was down where I could reach it, and later, on days when Joe was in bed or something, I heated soup and made fried-egg sandwiches for him. Also tea and coffee.

4

When I went home for lunch Dad was there and insisted on putting iodine on my scrape. By that time it had clotted over enough so the iodine didn't burn hardly at all, but I was outraged anyway and just about had kittens. Dad's pretty easygoing most of the time but he has the kind of temper that flares up, Voom. When he loses his temper he makes all kinds of sweeping rules and regulations and then has to take them back a couple of hours later when he's had a chance to cool off. I have the same kind of temper and that day we both lost them.

I think the thing that made Dad so mad was not just that I was defying him, but to a large extent the fact that my close shave with the ebb current scared him. He always gets maddest when he's scared for us. The result was that Dad said I'd have to stay in the house for a solid week as punishment for having a tantrum. (He was having one too, but that doesn't count because when adults do it it isn't called a tantrum. Like teasing. When Uncle Otis does it it's called kidding and we're supposed to like it, but if Brock did it to me or vice-versa, we'd be in trouble for teasing and being mean.) Anyhow, when Dad said that I just about had a duck fit, and was so rude he added another week to my punishment.

He called from the office around four o'clock and said he realized he'd "over-done it" and let me off. But by then the afternoon was shot, so I didn't get to take Brock to Joe's with me that day as I'd planned. I took him Sunday afternoon instead, and Joe and Brock got on famously. Brock was intrigued by the fancy apparatus and asked a million questions, and Joe seemed to enjoy explaining and demonstrating, Joe even loosened up enough to show off a little for our admiration. He could chin himself with one hand. He'd just hook one hand over the bar and pull himself up his arm until his hand was level with his neck, smooth as butter. Either hand. Brock's been trying to do it ever since. No success so far.

Those first few weeks Joe went into town a lot. He had a lot of odds and ends to buy for the house. He had a special car with everything up where he could operate it by using just his hands so he could drive himself around. He'd wheel his chair up beside it, swing himself in, fold up the chair and stow it in the place for it, and off he'd go. He kept the car in a double pre-fab garage at the edge of his property.

Around here nobody gets accepted right off; there's a long period of watching, waiting and sizing up. That's why summer people hardly ever make it; they're simply not around long enough and besides there are so many of them they tend to blur together. But Joe obviously wasn't a summer person, and I suppose people made allowances because he was a cripple and a hero and all that stuff, so in general he was treated pretty well by everyone. And Joe was either good at names or else made a real effort, because he seemed to know nearly everyone's name by the end of a couple of weeks.

One of the first things he did was to get a library card. He couldn't go up the steps, of course, so he'd wait in his car while Miss Finch the librarian got his books for him and stamped his card and all. Miss Finch has light blonde hair (natural, not out of a bottle) and that year she was wearing it in a shoulder-length bob. She was always swinging it as she walked, and in between she sort of combed it into place with her fingers. That summer she was going steady with Marvin Potts and he liked pink so she wore pink all the time, which made her look like an ice-cream cone because she didn't get much of a tan sitting in the library all day.

Miss Finch and Joe got on like a house on fire from the first day they met. Miss Finch took to coming out the library door and down the steps like Loretta Young on TV, a big swirl of skirts and so forth. And Joe would sit there and look at her like a tomcat watching a canary. Then Miss Finch would lean down at the window of Joe's car, real lady-like and all that, but in such a way that he could see part way down her dress (she wore that kind of dress).

I thought Miss Finch was dopey and I was jealous of her flirting with Joe. When she was there I might as well have been invisible. After a couple of trips to the library, watching her lean all over Joe's car patting her hair and grinning, I got so mad I told Joe she wore falsies. It was true too. We kids knew about it because one day she lost the top of her bikini in a big wave at the beach. Joe just laughed at me and said he couldn't care less, that she was pretty. I said I didn't think she was all that pretty, that she had mud-colored eyes and a pointy nose. And I told him she wasn't really nice either, that he should just see how mean she was to us little kids, always making us wash our hands before touching a book. Joe said that she was right to make us wash our hands before handling books because otherwise the books would get all grubby. To point up his moral he took hold of my hands and turned them palm up and told me to look at them. They were grubby all right. I told him I still thought Miss Finch was a crab, and that I didn't care, so there. He laughed at me. Which made me so mad I left and didn't go back for two days.

When I did go back I'd forgotten all about it, and it took me a while to know what he meant when he asked me if all was forgiven. That's not true. I'd more or less forgotten, at least enough so it took me a second to catch on to what he meant, but I pretended to be far denser than necessary. I acted as if the entire conversation had vanished from my mind, which it hadn't. It's hard to remember the truth, especially when at the time you've put on an act that just about convinced yourself.

When you're eleven, a month is half as long as forever, and it seemed as if things had settled out into a wonderfully comfortable pattern. I liked having a place to go, besides just to play with the boys, and being with Joe made me feel important, as if the glamor of him being a dragon-slayer rubbed off a little bit on me. As I look back on it now I can begin to put things together and add up inflections and fleeting expressions that didn't mean much to me at the time, but were stored away for future reference. Now I can say that it was as if Joe had an artificial calmness about him. As if he was balanced on a narrow edge with liking the world on one side and disliking it on the other. As if somebody he respected had talked him into giving people a chance but he didn't really believe people were worth it, not deep down. The thing I did notice at the time was that there was something precarious and interesting about Joe, as if he was poised on the edge of decision. It was a little like being part-way through a book or a movie and not knowing which way the plot was going to turn. One way would lead to a happy ending and the other to a tragic one. There was suspense in knowing Joe, a tension.

Then one hot day with just a thin coolish breeze whispering in off the water, Mr. Felcon got over his hives and sallied forth to catch up on the gossip at the Lobster Pot. As he always does after a spell of hives, he then proceeded to get very busy. He'd had the visit to Joe St. George pending from when he first took to bed, so that was the first thing he did after seeing Mrs. Root.

We were in the yard with Joe when Mr. Felcon's mint-green Buick hove into view coming down the hill. Brock said, "Jeepers, look who's coming here!" and dived into the thicket of elderberry bushes.

Joe asked me who was coming; I said, "Mr. Felcon," added politely, "Excuse me," and joined Brock in the bushes, where I made myself comfortable and settled down to wait until Mr. Felcon went away.

We couldn't stand Mr. Felcon. Every time he got close enough to catch us, which wasn't often, believe me, and never happened if we saw him coming, he would get a death-grip on our upper arms and ask in that sticky voice of his, "And have you been good children?" And we'd find ourselves guiltily hanging our heads as if somebody had pushed a button. It was the darndest thing, and I've never figured out how he did it. Both Brock and I had fairly good opinions of ourselves. I don't mean to imply that we were conceited or anything, but we were aware of our virtues as well as our shortcomings. The thing about Mr. Felcon was that he had a knack of making us totally forget our virtues and remember only our shortcomings. Even if we knew we were averagely good children a second before he spoke, he had a talent for making us feel like beasts.

Probably because he thought we were. I suspect that Mr. Felcon's idea of a "good child" would be something fixed up by Mr. Dangerfield. (He's the undertaker and also does taxidermy for summer people.)

We always said yes we were good children. Once Brock said "No" just to see what would happen and the lecture that went with "No" was twice as long and twice as nauseating as the one that went with "Yes." Then Mr. Felcon would say, "Jesus was sad on Sunday when you didn't come to His house. Do you want to make Jesus sad?" and went on from there. I never had the nerve to say that I didn't think Jesus cared one way or the other, but I always wanted to. (I think Mr. Felcon must make Jesus want to vomit.)

So you can see why Brock and I wanted to avoid Mr. Felcon. He left his car in the parking area at the end of the road and came all the way round to the gate instead of stepping over one of the fallen sections of fence the way anybody else would have. Mr. Felcon, being militantly Protestant, doesn't wear a wrongside-to collar, but he tries to make up for it by wearing black suits and a city hat. It makes him look like a comic undertaker in a B-picture, especially since, whenever he's about to speak to someone, he purses up his mouth as if he's thinking about sucking a lemon.

He came across Joe's yard mincingly, looking down and picking his way like a man in a chicken run. I think he was trying not to get sand in his shoes, but he gave the impression of a man trying not to step on something nasty.

He was so busy watching where he was stepping he didn't look up at Joe until he got up close and stopped. A horrified expression slid onto his face and slid right off again as he got hold of himself. His eyes flicked over Joe's face once more and came to rest on the top button of Joe's Hawaii shirt. Joe's neck acquired a noticeable pulse when he caught Mr. Felcon's initial reaction, but he didn't say anything except "Hello."

Mr. Felcon took off his hat and hung on to it as if it would keep him from sinking. He put on a smile and said, "May I introduce myself? I am Mr. Felcon." He didn't say it loudly or anything, but he made it sound as if he thought he was the King of Spain.

Joe introduced himself and put out his hand. Mr. Felcon sort of brushed his fingertips across the palm by way of a handshake and grabbed his hat again. I could see that Joe didn't like it, but Mr. Felcon didn't see because he was still looking intently at Joe's button.

Mr. Felcon then launched into his standard welcoming speech, which is pretty nauseating so I won't go into it. It is studded with references to "Our Fair Village" and "Friendly Populace" and it ends with a hard-sell pitch for his church services, a "Jesus is sad" routine on the adult level. It's a fairly long speech and halfway through I noticed that Joe was yawning with his mouth closed. Mr. Felcon still was addressing Joe's shirt button though, so he didn't see.

Mr. Felcon's speech bored me too and I nearly jumped out of my skin when Brock suddenly jabbed me in the ribs. I automatically jabbed him back, but instead of doing it back again, Brock put his finger to his lips for silence and pointed up the hill. Coming down the road with his swinging three-legged trot was Adonis. It was not surprising to see him there; he ranged all over the place and he'd been to visit Joe on several occasions. My first thought was that I hoped he wouldn't come over to the bushes to greet us and give us away, then I saw him reach Mr. Felcon's car, pause and sniff. He nosed around it a moment, then followed Mr. Felcon's scent all the way around the fence to the gate. He was wagging his tail and grinning. Some dogs do grin, you know.

Brock and I looked at Mr. Felcon. He wasn't expecting Adonis and he was standing smack in the middle of the yard with his back to the gate. Joe must have seen Adonis, but I don't think he knew about Adonis and Mr. Felcon, so he ignored the dog. Mr. Felcon was just winding up his pitch for his church when Adonis came up behind him and goosed him.

Mr. Felcon yelped and jumped about three feet straight up into the air. When he came down again he was off-balance so when Adonis rose up to embrace him, he fell down on his hands and knees. Adonis hadn't had a chance like that since Old Man Peel's funeral, and he made the most of it.

Then Joe began to laugh. He laughed until his face was red, the veins stood out on his temples and his scars stayed white so they showed three times as much as

53

usual. It wasn't the laugh he came to use later, there was some genuine amusement in it, but it was unpleasant, and also whenever Joe laughed loudly there was a metallic quality that made it sound even worse. I wonder if perhaps the steel prosthesis in his mouth caused that. Brock and I were shocked to the core. Nobody laughed at Mr. Felcon; it was like kicking a man when he's down, or laughing at a cripple. Maybe deep down inside we all thought it was funny, maybe we related the times it happened and laughed, but that doesn't mean we'd have laughed aloud right in Mr. Felcon's face. Joe didn't even try to call Adonis off or anything, he just sat there and bellowed.

Mr. Felcon had an awful time getting up. Adonis is an unusually big collie and he had a good grip around Mr. Felcon's waist with his forelegs. Finally Mr. Felcon managed to get to his feet though. He and Adonis began doing a sort of little dance; Adonis kept trying to circle around to get behind Mr. Felcon and Mr. Felcon was determined to keep Adonis in front of him and at the same time wanted to get back to his car. They waltzed around the yard, Mr. Felcon limping a little from having twisted his ankle and Adonis grinning and limping, as always, with his off hind-leg. He was wagging his tail and panting with his tongue out. Just about the time Mr. Felcon got to the gate Joe stopped laughing a minute to yell, "Try washing your underwear why don't you?"

Mr. Felcon turned pea-green and sort of galloped crabwise to his car. He got in, slammed the door in Adonis's face, and took off in a cloud of dust. Adonis trotted patiently off after the car.

54

After a couple of minutes Joe stopped laughing and called to us, "You can come out now."

We came out and walked over to him, not saying a word. We disapproved violently of his laughing and of what he'd said and it showed all over our faces.

Joe looked at us and demanded, "What's eating you? I thought you didn't like him."

"We don't," Brock said, "but that was mean."

"You shouldn't have said that," I added.

"Or laughed at him right in his face," Brock finished.

"Well, well," Joe said sarcastically, "Don't you make a nice little half-pint judge and quarter-pint jury?"

"It wasn't nice," Brock said with that bland immovable stubbornness he sometimes shows. When he's like that you could kill him before he'd back down an inch. He doesn't get mad or anything, he just goes blank and won't budge.

"Neither is your Mr. Felcon very nice," Joe said.

"Never said he was," Brock said. "But him not being nice doesn't entitle you not to be."

I stood there with my mouth ajar. Here was Brock sounding like an adult and Joe sounding like a kid, and Brock actually seemed to be facing Joe down. I glanced towards the causeway and saw Mr. Felcon's car crossing it at a good clip. The mint-green Buick turned down the main street and a moment later parked beside the Lobster Pot.

There's a saying, "You shouldn't kick a man when he's down because he might get up again." It occurred to me that Mr. Felcon could be a very nasty customer when riled. He'd certainly get even with Joe somehow. His brand of Christianity doesn't include forgiveness as

55

one of the "musts." He's the kind of Christian (there are a lot of them) that doesn't smoke, drink, dance, or approve of sex; that avoids slothfulness and similar sins, and by the time such a person has done all that—he think's he done enough. Perhaps the most unfortunate result is that people who deny themselves fun are then able to feel superior to everyone who does have fun, and this leads to self-righteousness. Mom says self-righteousness is the eighth deadly sin. Anyway, Mr. Felcon is vindictive as the devil.

Brock was still standing there like a guilty conscience staring at Joe. Joe was looking uncomfortable. I said, thinking about Mr. Felcon, "He'll fix your wagon for that."

Joe was delighted to have me change the subject. He gave me his attention. "What could that little pipsqueak do to me?" he asked. "I could break him in half with one hand."

I didn't doubt that he could, but I knew Mr. Felcon. "Don't be silly," I said. "He wouldn't get close enough to you for that. He'll do something sneaky."

"Like what?" Joe was amused.

"I don't know, but he'll think of something. You just wait and see."

Brock was still standing there glaring with his skinny arms folded across his chest in a very poor imitation of Dad when he's mad. Joe looked at him and began to laugh. Brock took hold of my arm and stated firmly, "We are going home."

He marched me out of the yard and up the road, with me yowling all the way because he was pinching a nerve. At the top of the hill he let go of me and snapped, "All right, shut off your noise!"

I rubbed my arm and sniffled. It really had hurt, and it kept on hurting a little bit, enough to remind me anyway. "I'm going back."

Brock glared at me then folded his arms again and said in a grand manner, "All right go!" He sounded like an irate father sending a fallen daughter out into a blizzard.

I sighed and gave up. "All right," I said meekly and docilely followed him on home. Brock was always doing that. He'd make some of the simplest situations into choices. He'd fix it so I was put in the position of having to choose between him and something or somebody else. It was all very phoney and silly in one way, like a week earlier when he had made the question of going down to the rocks or over to Bobby Wyddyn's a choice. The thing that made it not silly was that Brock was very serious about it and took my choices very much to heart. If I didn't choose him he acted betrayed for days after and wasn't fit to live in the same house with. He was always an expert on Meaningful Glances and stuff like that.

I generally gave in. I'm an expert on taking the easy way out (in fact that's one of my worst faults). So this time, like most of the others, I went along with Brock because it was easier and because I was already at the top of the hill and might as well; and then I spent the rest of the way home explaining to myself that going home was what I really wanted to do anyway. Now, I don't know if I wanted to go or stay. I don't know if going back to Joe would have made any difference at all. I expect it wouldn't have. I had planned to tell Joe he'd better apologize to Mr. Felcon, and I do think that if he had apologized things might have turned out differently. But I am also sure that Joe never would have agreed to apologize. Furthermore, he was a grown man and I certainly wasn't responsible for him. But even so, I wish I'd gone back and said my piece. Just for the record, just so I could know I'd done everything I could. I also wish I'd called out and warned Mr. Felcon of Adonis's arrival. I wish a whole lot of things.

While I'm at it it would make more sense to wish Mr. Felcon wasn't such a crummy person. It doesn't make sense to concentrate on what small sins of omission of mine might have contributed to the debacle, when there's no certainty that anything I could have done would have made a difference.

I wonder, is Mr. Felcon crummy because he likes to be or because he can't help it? Mom says that when a person becomes a caricature of himself, a travesty of what he might have been, that he's an object of pity. She says I should consider the kind of childhood such a person must have had for him to have become so warped. She believes that all people want to be good and human and whole, and that they suffer when they are not. I agree with her most of the time, but when I think of Mr. Felcon I wonder. He certainly acts as if he enjoys being horrid.

But if Mom's right, what then? Is it possible that Mr. Felcon sometimes sees himself for what he is? Sometimes in the night does he suffer to think back on the day and remember all the petty little meannesses he's committed? He must be aware that all the children in town hate him, that they walk behind him imitating his furtive walk, that they stick out their tongues and make a sign against the evil eye with forefinger and little finger when they think he's not looking, that they run away when they see him approaching. Does he hate children because he can see in their faces that they hate and fear him? When a dog cringes when you come near, it can make you want to kick it; is that why he bullies children?

He has his little circle of admirers, but he would have to be very stupid not to know that his gaggle of pet gossips is nearly as unpopular as he is. Is it possible that he doesn't *know* why everyone avoids him? Is it possible that he doesn't know how he sounds to others? How painful it would be to walk through life being avoided and ridiculed behind one's back and never know why. Does he try TV remedies? Bad breath pills, mouth-washes, deodorants and medicated soaps? Does he dream of walking out one morning to have people greet him with enthusiasm and affection? Or does he see people's attitudes as a flaw in them instead of in himself?

Anyway, whatever his reasons, whatever his motives, Mr. Felcon very promptly proceeded to get even with Joe. I don't know exactly what happened but it is a fact that he spent most of the afternoon talking to Mrs. Root. I asked around about that afternoon, and this is what I found out: It was a slow day at the Lobster Pot, as are most days out of season. There was a young couple who had just rented a shore cottage from Mr. O'Connor who came in looking for knicknacks to put in it. They bought a pair of candles stuck into corks and one of those glass Japanese floats that Mrs. Root buys from California. There was a woman looking for bargain antiques, but she didn't buy anything.

Mr. Goodfellow's cousin Fred, who is a carpenter, came in around three to fix Mrs. Root's window-frame and Mr. Felcon left. I don't know what Mr. Felcon told

Mrs. Root, but I'm sure of one thing: he didn't mention Adonis. He has never admitted Adonis exists. Maybe he hopes that if he ignores him hard enough he'll go away. I can imagine Mr. Felcon and Mrs. Root talking, I've seen them often enough. Mrs. Root would have been listening intently, nodding agreement from time to time. Mr. Felcon would have been rocking on his heels as I'm told he does in his church, and expounding with elocutionary gestures with a slightly condescending expression on his face. He must have had a lot to say that afternoon.

At three-fifteen Mrs. Root asked Fred Goodfellow if he'd keep an eye on the shop and went out to buy a bottle of aspirin (anyhow, that's what she told Fred she was going to do). While she was in the drugstore waiting for Mr. St. Laurent to wrap the aspirin she told him in her very carrying voice that Mr. Felcon had had an "appalling" experience.

Mr. St. Laurent said, "You don't say," in a tone that closed the conversation and indicated total disbelief.

The gaggle of gossips was there at their table though, as they always are around that time of day, and they heard what Mrs. Root said. The hard core of the group, the fringes of which vary according to the state of certain long-standing local feuds, are Granger, Thornton, Page, and McNutt, Inc. (as Dad refers to them so they sound like a firm of lawyers). Miss McNutt is the thin one, Mrs. Granger has a henpecked husband, Mrs. Thornton is a widow and the saying locally is that she drove her husband to drink when he was alive, Mrs. Page is also a widow and she has purple hair (she uses a rinse). Granger, Thornton, and Page are all very fat and pishy and sort of overflow Mr. St. Laurent's bent-

60

wood chairs. Miss McNutt sort of perches as if the seat was too hard.

They sit there for about an hour every afternoon eating cake and sticky buns and drinking tea and gossiping. I've overheard them lots of times. Mrs. Granger specializes in death, doctors, and diseases. She diagnoses and second-guesses doctors. She's had about a dozen operations (Doc Elsinger told Dad once that most, if not all, of them were unnecessary. How is that possible?) and she talks about her operations if nothing new is going on. Thornton and Page specialize in romance, marriage, and the worthlessness of men, and when they run out of fresh gossip they fall back on their alternately Dear-Departed and worthless husbands, depending. The three who have been married sometimes band together to annoy Miss McNutt by implying one way and another that an unmarried woman isn't really a woman. Miss McNutt counter-attacks by implying that chastity is the only really worthwhile virtue, and by talking at some length about her Dear-Departed-Papa, who was, according to her, the living end. She also quotes back to Thornton and Page some of the things they've said about their worthless husbands, slides in a few references to the gossip that Thornton drove her husband to drink, and points out to Granger, whose operations include a hysterectomy, that she can hardly call herself a woman. Granger then says that it isn't what you have that counts so much as how you make use of it. And it goes on like that. Summers they can spend their time criticizing summer people and things aren't too bad, but by the end of a long, dull winter and spring they are at each other's throats like four tomcats in a barrel. The less gossip there is the more they rub each other

61

the wrong way, and they all know each other well enough to be able to make each other livid with a flick of a phrase.

The day in question Mrs. Root hadn't had a chance to turn around before they surrounded her demanding the details of Mr. Felcon's misfortune. They practically dragged Mrs. Root to their table where they plied her with tea and buns and set about trying to extract the story. Which wasn't hard since that was what she'd gone there for in the first place. But she wanted to make them work for it so she held out for half an hour before admitting grudgingly that something really appalling had happened to Mr. Felcon. Which they knew already but which made them relax because they knew that Mrs. Root was preparing-to-tell. There are certain rules that must be observed in passing on gossip, and one of them is that the purveyor of information has to feel that the information was forced out of her. You can't just go up and say "What's new?" and expect to be told. The reply to that is, "Oh nothing, except. . . ." You are then expected to beg to be told what the "except" refers to, and bit by bit you drag it out, each question leading to a reply that tells something but not all and has a hook in it leading you on to your next question. I think the point is to make the suspense last as long as possible. It's like a game.

Anyway, Mrs. Root after much prodding admitted that the appalling thing had happened to Mr. Felcon at the old Prescott place. At this juncture there was time out to rehash the antique gossip about the Prescott family. After the Prescotts were exhausted Mrs. Root admitted that Joe St. George had done something appalling. She never did come out and say what the appalling thing was, but she hinted broadly around and around. Because she wouldn't say specifically she left the impression that it was something too hideous to be mentioned. Naturally the gossips assumed that if Mrs. Root wouldn't say what it was, it had to be something really extraordinarily awful. Apparently it never occurred to them that Mrs. Root either didn't know exactly what happened (which is likely considering that Mr. Felcon never would have mentioned Adonis) or had nothing to tell.

With no facts to trammel their imaginations the gossips had a field-day, and the story got denser, murkier, and more awful as it went. All hints, you understand. There was a good deal of discussion and speculation revolving around Joe's war experiences and the general agreement they arrived at was that his mind had been affected and he was some sort of maniac. Even though the appalling thing was supposed to have happened to Mr. Felcon they arrived at the conclusion that Joe was a menace to women and children.

Somewhere in here Miss Finch got into the act and, being given to hysterics, promptly had them. Marvin Potts just happened to be nearby (which no doubt gave her more of an incentive for hysterics) and drove her home. This turned into a habit because they took to necking at the far edge of the salt marsh, and for a while it looked as if they were going to have to get married, but Miss Finch took a trip to New York to "visit relatives" and Marvin simply took off, so Miss Finch is still unmarried after all. It's sort of sad.

The gossip didn't last long. I think it only lasted as long as it did because of Mrs. Root's reputation as a source of accurate and up-to-the-minute news. And probably Joe's face had something to do with it too. It's much easier to believe evil of an ugly or deformed person than of a whole and handsome one. Perhaps the fact he was living at the old Prescott place had some influence, because there's a very real history of evil connected to that house. And Joe was something of a mystery in town; nobody knew him well enough to be able to say "Oh nonsense" right off.

The next day Dad asked us about it; he'd heard it from a couple of patients (you'd be surprised how much talking people can do with their mouths full of fingers) and he knew we visited Joe. We told about Adonis and everything, and he told a couple of people and that was the end of that. Everybody had a good laugh about Mr. Felcon's problem with Adonis. But it took a couple of days for the story to make a full circuit and get back to Miss Finch and by that time it was too late.

5

"What is so rare as a day in June, if ever come perfect days . . ." (to quote Uncle Otis). Well, the day Joe discovered he was *persona non grata* with Miss Finch was a rare day all right. It was also perfect, if you're thinking about weather. The sky was blue as a postcard, with gulls floating high up like scraps of paper, the sun was warm and golden, and the sea was sparkling, ruffled by a good steady breeze. All the sailboats were out and far off over the horizon the Navy was having target practice and we could hear the regular thud of big guns, like distant thunder.

Brock decided he wanted to buy a kite and talked me into going with him into the village, which is what we were doing there. Brock always agonizes over choices. He must have spent the better part of an hour trying to decide if he wanted a paper kite or a plastic one, then after deciding on paper he couldn't make up his mind if he wanted red, yellow, or blue. I'd bought a box of colored chalk within the first five minutes and spent the rest of the time sitting on the floor by the magazine rack reading comic books (the store owner wouldn't let you read comic books unless you had a reason to be in there and we weren't allowed to buy them because they're trash, so I was perfectly happy with Brock's indecision that day). Finally Brock bought a red kite with a picture of a rocket on it, I skimmed the rest of the comic I was reading to see how Batman got out of the concrete underground dungeon, and followed Brock out. Just as I got out onto the sidewalk, I heard Joe's car horn. Joe was parked in front of the library waiting for Miss Finch to come out.

Brock wanted to see if we could get a ride part-way home, so we started over toward the car. Miss Finch was taking an awfully long time about coming out I thought; apparently Joe thought so too, because he honked his horn again, more insistently. He already had that hungry look on his face.

Then Miss Finch appeared. I noticed right off that she made her entrance differently, more Bishop Sheen than Loretta Young. Skirts swirling, but stiff, on her dignity. She had a haughty glassy look on her face, and she was deliberately not looking at Joe.

I glanced at Joe; he still had that eager look on his face, but he looked a bit puzzled as if he was wondering if he had offended her somehow. As we got close, she hove up beside the car and, looking icily into the distance, was giving him the deep-freeze treatment. She'd resurrected an old library rule that said one had to have been a resident of the village for two years before one could take out a book. This rule was news to Brock and me; it had never, to our knowledge, been enforced. In fact, even mentioning it was arrant nonsense. All a summer person has to do to get a book is to walk into the library, put down a five-dollar deposit (because so many of them forget to return books at the end of the season) and sign his name.

Miss Finch was being so polite I wanted to slap her and Joe's look of anticipation and happiness had faded to a look of stricken incredulity. He obviously hadn't the faintest idea why she was acting like that, and his feelings were badly hurt.

Miss Finch was going on and on about this antediluvian rule, justifying herself and so forth. Joe reached out his hand, very gently and slowly, and touched her arm, and asked, "Why are you mad at me?"

She flinched away as if he was contagious and continued her spiel about an octave higher and somewhat louder. She ended up taking the books he was returning and saying that she would get his deposit and return it to him, then she went pounding up the steps and back into the library leaving Joe sitting there looking stunned.

Brock grabbed me by the wrist and took off after her, dragging me in his wake. He had that bland, stubborn look on his face.

Brock went straight up to the tall desk inside the library. He could barely see over the top, but he rapped authoritatively for attention. Miss Finch had been fussily rooting around in the petty cash box looking for the five dollars. She jumped a foot and turned around, then she leaned over the desk and scowled down at us. I edged around behind Brock, but he stood his ground and glared up at her.

"You'll have to wait, children," she snapped.

"That was downright mean," Brock announced forcefully. "You ought to be ashamed."

This took her aback. She blinked, fluttered her hands the way she does, and opened and shut her mouth a couple of times. Then she collected herself and said snappily, pulling rank on Brock, "Mind your own business Brock Brewer, or I'll tell your father on you."

"You just go right ahead and do that," Brock said inexorably. I was appalled at his daring, practically shaking in my shoes, but he didn't seem in the least scared. "I'm going to tell Marvin Potts you wear falsies," he added.

She turned red as a cooked lobster and began fluttering worse than ever. "You wouldn't!"

Brock didn't say anything to this, he just stood there in his guilty-conscience pose and waited, staring at her like a basilisk. Just looking at him anyone could tell that he would do exactly what he said.

Miss Finch fluttered and squeaked for a while, and finally gave up and asked in a real little voice but trying to make it sound authoritative (it didn't), "What do you want, you nasty boy?"

"I want you to treat Mr. St. George the way you ought," Brock said promptly.

Miss Finch shook her head and began blithering about Joe being a "positive maniac" and other such nonsense that doesn't bear repeating. It looked to me as if Brock was being outclassed and out-talked. He'd shot his wad and didn't have anything left to threaten her with. It was clear that an appeal to her better self wasn't going to work since she apparently didn't have a better self. I was standing there wondering how to help Brock and Miss Finch was working up her courage yelling at him, when all of a sudden I remembered the box of new colored chalk in my pocket. I took it out and removed the red piece. I think I must have grinned because Miss Finch stopped hollering for a moment and shot me a very odd look.

I handed the chalk to Brock. He caught on immediately. He held it up in all its pristine newness to show her and she stopped talking to stare at it. Brock said very calmly and politely, "If you don't treat Mr. St. George the way you ought, we'll write 'Miss Finch wears falsies' all over town." He began writing it out in the air in front of him in foot-high letters.

"The box has yellow, green, blue, and brown in it too," I said helpfully. "And orange," I added as an afterthought, after a glance at the box.

The idea of it being written in all those colors caved her in, at least she seemed to give up somewhere around blue. "All right, all right!" she said, "Whatever you say." She was looking at us as if we each had two heads.

She went off muttering to herself about juvenile crime-waves and blackmail, but she got Joe the book he'd asked for, took it down to him, and marked his card. We followed right after, and she kept glancing at us and edging away from us as if she expected us to bite. She even, after a look at us, remembered to apologize for dredging up that old rule. But she wouldn't tell Joe why she'd put the freeze on him and she didn't take the freeze off. She was icy-polite, and didn't go too near the car, reaching out at arm's length with the book.

After Miss Finch marked his card, Joe didn't reach out far enough for it so, far away as she was standing, she teetered and had difficulty handing it back to him.

He looked at her and began to laugh. That was the first time we heard that particular laugh that was to become so characteristic of him. I was going to call it his new laugh, but though it was new to us, I am convinced that it wasn't new for him. It was as humorless and hostile as a punch in the nose. When he began laughing Miss Finch bolted. She was in such a rush she tripped on the top step and fell flat on her face and ran her stockings. That made Joe laugh louder and harder than ever.

Brock looked at me and shrugged his shoulders. I did the same thing. We'd done all we could; it wasn't our fault things hadn't turned out well. Brock handed me back my piece of red chalk, I put it back in the box, put the box in my pocket, and we went off home by way of the seawall, not waiting to see about a ride. I don't think Joe noticed us leaving, he was still looking up the library steps after Miss Finch who had disappeared inside.

Don't get the idea that other people in town acted like Miss Finch, because they didn't. They treated him exactly the same as before. Even Mrs. Root treated him all right. She'd sell her grandmother to Dracula if she could turn two cents by the deal, and she was selling Joe's bottled ships for five times what she paid him.

Joe forced the town to dislike him. After his little set-to with Miss Finch he began laughing at everyone, and it was a mean, hard laugh that made him sound like a maniac. How can a person carry on a conversation with someone who's laughing like a hyena, and loud too? It wasn't long before people stopped trying to talk to Joe, even Mr. St. Laurent who is the soul of patience.

So, while there's no doubt that Mr. Felcon and Mrs. Root started the whole thing, there's also no doubt that it wouldn't have amounted to a hill of beans if Joe hadn't seen fit to keep it going, if he hadn't seized on the excuse to turn people away from him. It was almost as if he'd been waiting for a single good solid excuse for acting like that, and once he had it he wasn't going to let it go to waste.

Why should a man want to be a pariah? Did Joe really want to be or was it that he could never believe that people could stand looking at him, so he was more comfortable in the middle of honest hostility than what he considered phoney goodwill? As I look back, he was somewhat more relaxed after he began laughing at people, as if he'd gotten out of a Sunday suit and into clothes that fit.

I've read that when a man has a bad face wound, the doctors and staff won't let him see a mirror until after they've had a chance to fix it up some. Did Joe manage to find some reflecting surface too early in the game, a polished tray or a window with night behind it, or perhaps some shiny metal bowl that distorted his image like a fun-house mirror? Did he look and laugh? Laugh like the damned because he knew he'd never look quite human again? Did he look into people's eyes and see his reflection in their pupils? There were no mirrors in his house, not even a shaving mirror. He shaved by feel with an electric razor.

Did he learn to laugh like that in order to spit in the face of despair when the plastic surgeons took off the bandages and saw the enormous scars, when they tried x-rays (as they must have) and discovered that all the skill of medicine couldn't smooth away the damage because every hair-thin cut developed into a rope of keloid tissue? Did he laugh at his doctors, as if by laughing he could make it seem their fault? Or maybe make them so angry at him that they wouldn't blame themselves too much because all their skill and patience hadn't been enough?

I think that's one reason people took to avoiding him. His laughter was bad enough in terms of sheer noise, but beside the hostility there was a quality of despair about it that made Joe seem to be their fault. It was an accusation as well as an assault and when they were accused they were guilty and didn't know why. He was like the unburied dead come back to haunt the wrong house. Even if they knew it was the wrong house, the very fact of his presence made them doubt, made them wonder if perhaps they were more guilty than they had supposed, and ask themselves if this uneasy ghost had a reason not clear to them but nevertheless real.

The trouble was that people couldn't help wishing he was dead. They couldn't help thinking that it would have been better for everybody if he had died in Korea rather than come back half-killed to shadow the sunlit summer. I've heard various people say at various times, in various ways, "For his own sake, it's a pity he didn't die." So if they couldn't help killing him mentally over and over again, how could they forgive him for that? Once he was one hundred per cent dead they could forgive him, perhaps even love him after a fashion. At least they could appreciate his heroism. I don't agree with Brock that the flowery obit and eulogies were flagrant phoneyness; I think that people really were sorry he was dead.

I keep speaking of "they" as if I'd had no share in

the village's opinion of Joe, but that wouldn't be quite true. It is true that I kept going to see him, and was good friends with him, but I couldn't stand his laugh either and I think that if he'd used it on me even once I might never have gone back. He did laugh at me quite often, and not necessarily kindly, but he didn't use that particular public laugh. He didn't do it to Brock either.

Both Brock and I explained what had happened, how Miss Finch had got herself in an uproar over what the gossips said, and all that. We also told him to stop laughing at people and very carefully tried to explain that he was being obnoxious, but he laughed at us. Not the public laugh, but bad enough. So he knew what he was doing and he was told too. He never denied doing it on purpose, and he kept right on doing it after we'd explained.

Around that time a cat got into the garage and damaged one of Brock's mice. It was getting on towards dusk and beginning to be too chilly for comfort. The street-lights were on and the tree by the end of the driveway cast long swinging shadows across the yard and side of the house and garage. The light from the garage spilled out the open door sidelighting the pebbles in the driveway so they looked like something out of a surrealist painting.

Brock captured the damaged mouse, which had run under the table, and examined her. There was bright red blood on the end of her nose, lung blood, and we both knew she was going to die.

"What do you think, Jessica?" Brock said.

I shook my head, to indicate that the mouse had had it.

The mouse sort of twitched and he said in a suffering voice, "It hurts her." Then all of a sudden he was frantic. He looked around with his eyes showing white and spied a shovel in the corner. He put the mouse, which was already dying, down on the edge of the concrete just outside the garage door and belted her with the shovel. He nearly squashed her flat but she kept twitching. He belted her again and again, saying *Please* die, please." Tears were practically squirting out of his eyes.

When the mouse was finally dead he picked up the remains, and believe me, not much remained, and went out into the dark to bury them. I made a move to follow but he motioned to me to stay put so I did. It was his funeral after all, and I had no business intruding. I could hear him weeping in the dark while he dug a hole with the same shovel. I never felt sorrier for anyone in my life.

After that Brock bought some cyanide at the drugstore and made a cyanide bottle with plaster of Paris and a quart jar. I must say it's a lot more humane, at least for the murderer. I don't know how the mice feel about it.

The next day Brock saw the cat that had done it and began throwing rocks at it. Then all of sudden he stopped short just as he was about to throw another one and instead of heaving it at the cat, dropped it on the ground and said, "What the hell, why take it out on the cat?"

"Isn't that the same cat?" I asked.

"Yeh, but it's not her fault she's a cat. A cat can't help acting like a cat any more than a mouse can help being edible. She was only doing what cats are supposed to do."

74

Of course he was right.

That's the trouble with the thing about Joe. It would be so much more comfortable and easy to go ahead and pin the blame somewhere, anywhere. But by the time you've thought about it a while you end up not able to blame anyone, not even yourself. You can say, "If this had happened this way instead of that, then . . ." but the trouble is that ahead of time you don't know that a certain happening is the choice-point. That's something you only find out when you look back. Well, as Dad says, "It's a shame our foresight isn't as good as our hindsight."

Brock says that he kept on visiting Joe at least partly because he was sorry for him. I don't think I was as sorry for him as all that, though I do remember hurting for him when Miss Finch froze him. But I'm always hurting for people so that doesn't necessarily signify. I'm not kidding, it's a real problem, and I've got it so bad that when a comic starts telling mother-in-law jokes all I can do is worry if he's hurting his mother-in-law's feelings. It's ridiculous.

Brock has it even worse than I do. He even went on a vegetarian kick last year and stuck to it for three whole months because he couldn't stand the thought of people killing lambs and nice brown-eyed cows and things. I never could see the point of it all; after all, lambs and cows and hogs are going to be slaughtered whether Brock eats them or not, so why not enjoy meat?

What got my goat about Brock and the meat was that he tried to make me do it too, and gave out with that old line about, "If everybody did it, then . . . etc." Which is ridiculous because it's clearly apparent that everybody etc. darn well won't. Besides, I like meat and

75

I hate to think the kind of mess it would be if an omnivorous species like people had to stop eating it. As a matter of fact, the thing that made Brock come to his senses was when the mice, whom he had put on a meat-free diet, began eating each other. Mice tend to do that from time to time anyway, they're naturally cannibalistic but by the end of three months without even dry dogfood, they were going to it with real enthusiasm and he lost two litters, a few adults, and had trouble meeting his monthly quota for the lab. Mom was very patient about Brock's anti-meat kick, and gave him cheese and eggs (unfertilized). After a while you could tell by the look on Brock's face that he could hardly stand the sight of either one. I remember one day, when he was about to take his first reluctant bite of an omelette, I leaned over and whispered, "Through the lips and over the gums, look out stomach! Here it comes!" and he darn near killed me. So much for principles of nonviolence. But to tell the truth, I'd never been silly enough to think for a minute that they applied to siblings.

That's an odd thing, stop to think of it. Does a diet deficient in meat make people mean? It sure made Brock mean. Or is there a basic cruelty in people that's bound to come out one way or another? Down at the A.S.P.C.A. they won't give puppies or kittens to families with children under two because they have the notion that children under two are too mean to animals (do they think a second birthday is magic?). But if they haven't unloaded their excess puppies and kittens in a week they gas them, and if that isn't mean I don't know what is. They're also crazy about castrating animals and do it to all the cats they get their hands on, and I don't see what's so kind about that. How do they think the cats feel? (I remember Mom said once that they belong to the anti-life faction. I think she's right.)

I wish people would be more consistent. Heck, I wish *I* would be more consistent. Mom says life would be pretty dull if you always knew what to expect, but I still think that a little more consistency wouldn't hurt any. If only people would act the way they talk, or talk the way they act instead of so often saying one thing and doing the exact opposite.

And let's face it, for all my tender-heartedness I can be as mean as anyone sometimes. And I'm not necessarily sorry afterwards either. So maybe I shouldn't be so hard on Miss Finch. Maybe she honestly was scared of Joe. I know that if you put on a good enough act you can end up convincing yourself, and Miss Finch was never a giant brain, so who knows? There's a good chance that she really believed Joe was some kind of maniac, in which case I ought to be sorry we blackmailed her into treating him like a person. I'm not sorry though.

6

Horseshoe crabs are fascinating to read about but exceedingly boring to watch. About the only interesting thing they do is to turn up in June with a big one carrying a whole row of smaller ones on its tail, like train cars. For ages I thought that it was a mother with babies but Joe told me that the little ones are males and the big one is female. I wonder what the old ladies who exclaim over such maternal devotion would think of that? Someday I'll have to tell one and see.

Joe said that they swim wrong side up (the crabs, that is, not the old ladies) but I've never seen one swimming, only plowing around in the mud at low tide. The very little ones are pale blue but the big ones are all brown. They have compound eyes like bugs, and their shells are made of the kind of shell-stuff bugs are made of, slightly flexible, not out of the hard stony shell-stuff real crabs are made of.

We used to go down to the mud flats to catch them sometimes, but they're too easy to catch; you just walk up and pick one up by the tail, which is a rigid spike. They hinge at the base of the tail and between the head and middle section, but not enough to close up or anything. Once you've caught one there isn't much you can do with it except carry it around, they're too big to fit in a pail, being around a foot or more long, and they don't bite or pinch or anything. We used to tell the summer people's kids that the tails were poisoned and scare them, which was fun, but not all that much. The thing that always puzzled me, and still does, is where they keep their insides. They're all hollow under that big round head, and even inside their shells they seem to be empty; there doesn't seem to be any place for them to keep a stomach or heart or any of those other things animals need to live. The double row of flat plates under the middle section are book gills. Joe said that they're analogous to spiders' book lungs, but I never saw anything on a spider that looks remotely like that. Spiders must keep them someplace inside. Joe showed me how horseshoe crabs' mouths open sideways right between the two rows of legs, and said that they chew with the bases of their legs. Joe knew a lot about all kinds of things. He told me all this the day I brought him a huge horseshoe crab to see. He also said they were living fossils, that they were more than 150 million years old, and that it was a mystery how they'd survived all that time without changing.

We were out in the yard that day. Joe spent a lot of time outside when it was sunny; he seemed to like sunshine, more than I do, in fact. I remember saying that I didn't see how it was such a mystery. They aren't fit to eat (as far as I know there's nothing that eats them) and that I thought a good design would stand the test

79

of time. I mean, what's so strange about animals turning up with a few really good designs early in the game? Like sharks.

Joe wheeled over nearer the water's edge and heaved the crab in before it died. He said that he thought I had a point, that maybe the strange thing was that other animals *hadn't* survived, not that some had.

That year the boys were given a dory to fool around with. A dory is not a rowboat, though it is small enough to row. They are fishing boats, and still used by fishermen off the Grand Banks. Dories are exceedingly seaworthy, sturdy, almost impossible to sink. You can step a small mast and sail them if you have to or want to. They are pointed at both ends with flat bottoms; the ones used for mossing have a square removable pen in the middle to hold the seaweed. The boys were also helped to build three lobster pots and they renovated two others we'd found on the rocks not too badly stove in. The boys weren't going to let me in on it, but they found out that I was better at making nets than any of them so they decided I could be sort of an honorary boy. Lobster traps need three conical nets. There are two leading into the outer part of the trap, they are fastened with the wide part toward the outside and the narrow end, which is tied in place and kept open with a wire ring, on the inside. The trap is divided in two by a partition with a hole in it, with the third net leading in to the bait. Once the lobsters get inside they can't get out again because the narrow end of the funnel is too small for them to crawl into. The traps are made of narrow wooden slats, with a lid that opens, and they are weighted with a brick in each corner of the bottom.

The boys wanted to be different from anyone else, so

instead of painting their floats red, yellow, orange, white or black like everyone else, they painted them sky-blue. Of course, if they had thought about it for one whole minute they'd have realized why nobody else had sky-blue floats. They had a horrible time locating them. Then they put on orange stripes and that took care of that. Each person has his own float pattern and color combination. J. Wyddyn, for instance, has bright yellow with two black bands; Oakley's father has white with a red end, and so on. My mother's father had red ones with a white band. There are still a couple of them hanging up in the toolshed.

Unfortunately a lot of the lobsters you catch are shorts. (That means smaller than the legal limit.) The men throw the shorts back, but the boys didn't—unless they saw somebody's father approaching. The boys had an extra problem because all the best locations for traps were already taken, and you can't go putting your traps in somebody else's territory. It just isn't done. So just about all they got was shorts. We'd put them in a burlap sack and take them to the two-acre poison ivy patch behind the coast-guard station. There was a hidden path through the ivy into a clear sandy place right smack in the middle. There we'd made a sort of fireplace (the rocks kept splitting and we kept having to replace them) using a piece of metal grill the boys had salvaged from the trash behind Poe's Garage. We used driftwood and cooked the lobsters in a pail of sea water. We never bothered to peg their claws so somebody had to stand by the pail with a stick and shove them back in when they tried to climb back out. After they were cooked we sat around and ate them, then we took the shells and burned them under the rocks at the shoreline where the game warden wouldn't find them. At first we'd just thrown them into the ivy but after a while the smell got to be too much for even kids and also there were flies.

The original idea had been to make a lot of money selling lobsters but, since we ate them all, it didn't work out that way. Sometimes we'd get a couple of legal-sized ones and sell them to our families or other people along the cliff, and we sold cooked legal ones to Joe for two dollars. He preferred getting them cooked and we thought it was easier to cook them than to whittle pegs for the claws, and adults are funny about having to shove their dinners back into the boiling water. Whenever we got only one legal one we'd take it to Joe after we'd cooked it with our own. His house was just down the hill from the poison ivy; we could see it from our fireplace if we stood up.

Now the poison ivy patch isn't there any more. Somebody bought it, put on weed-killer, bulldozed it, and has it all laid out for a housing development, with a street and everything. Poison ivy is already beginning to sprout around the piles of bricks and sand though; it isn't all that easy to get rid of poison ivy.

We also used to cook clams up there. Most of our local mud flats are too squashy for clams, so adults never bother with them. In most places you sink halfway to your knees and usually end up getting cut on the broken razor-shell clamshells in the mud. But we kids knew where the few firm-enough patches were, and we could dig a good helping of quahogs at low tide. You tramp around on top of the mud and locate the clams when they squirt. There were also a few soft-shell clams which are good to eat, and we sometimes dug razor shells for bait. The hard part was leaving the clams in sea water overnight to get the mud out. There were times when we couldn't wait, but they were really much too muddy inside to be really enjoyable, so we finally learned patience. We cooked them in a pail of sea water, same as lobsters. Joe didn't like cooked clams, but he'd eat raw quahogs (which he called cherrystones) with lemon and katsup.

Summer people were always talking about clambakes, and I've read about them, but nobody around here ever baked a clam in seaweed. We'd always tell them that, and explain that steamed clams means boiled ones, but they never believed us. They'd go stumbling around down on the rocks gathering great clumps of seaweed and make an enormous mess, sometimes too far down so the incoming tide got them, and you could laugh yourself sick watching them raking around in hot, wet seaweed, seeing them jump when a rock split with a loud crack, or when an air bladder on the seaweed exploded. About an hour past dinner time when nothing was cooked yet and the kids were all crying from falling around on the rocks, they'd either give up completely or send somebody into the village for hotdogs. When they went away we'd go down and salvage the clams and whatever else there was. Usually the clams were only fit for bait by that time, but they made fine bait for flounders who like their food a little rotten.

Now that I look back on it, I wonder why we made such a big thing out of not whittling pegs for pegging lobsters. It isn't as time-consuming as being careful handling the lobsters is. I guess it was simply more fun to have the element of danger. Those New England lobsters can crush a finger if they get hold of one, and there was an element of skill involved in not getting pinched. You take hold of the lobster by the carapace just behind the base of the claws. It immediately reaches back as far as it can, so if you haven't got your arm at the right angle it can pinch your arm.

One time this show-offy summer kid wanted to hold a lobster and got his arm pinched. Like a dope he let go of it and of course it promptly grabbed a fold of his stomach with its other claw. The kid ran screaming all the way home and afterwards was mad at us. It wasn't our fault. We'd warned him and we'd showed him exactly how to do it, and besides, we'd lost the lobster because he took it home with him. It was a legal one, too, that we could have sold.

A couple of days later the kid, whose name was Horace, showed up with a couple of friends and went tramping around through everybody's Irish moss. Irish moss is little, crinkly seaweed. It's spread out to dry on the sand well above the tide line in rectangular patches. It bleaches from dark purple through shades of red to a cream-white. Then it's sold to a company that makes it into a kind of icky dessert called blanc-mange. I think British people eat it.

Anyway, we were up on the cliff flying kites that day and for one reason and another nobody else was around to see Horace and company lousing up the moss, so we went down to tell him to stop it, that after all you don't go stepping in somebody's way of making a living.

It turned out that Horace had brought his big brother and his big brother's friends, and we were outclassed but good. But we had a standard procedure for big, brassy summer kids. One of our games was to race each other across the rocks and we could run on them as fast as we could run on solid ground (it seemed faster, but I don't see how that's possible). The summer kids didn't have the trick though. It's a matter of timing and knowing just how to land and just how to take off, and how to pick the next rock and decide on a route three or four rocks ahead so you don't end up with no place to jump to. That day the tide was out, so we called Horace and company enough names (we were annoyed about that lobster and said Horace had stolen it and ought to pay for it) to get them all really mad, and then ran away. We started off across the rocks towards the low-tide mark, slow and clumsy like a mother bird playing broken-wing. They came after us and we kept them coming until they were way out where the seaweed grows. Then we began running circles around them and they were slipping and falling and getting cut up on barnacles. Finally they gave up and made their way back, just about crawling because by then they were afraid of the rocks, and we ran around and laughed at them. Now I can feel sorry for them; it must have been a nightmare to be led so far into a kind of terrain you can't cope with, but at the time I didn't feel sorry a bit.

Later that afternoon a delegation of fathers showed up; mad. They took a good look at us and compared our size to the size of Horace's brother and immediately calmed down. We explained very innocently that these kids had been stepping in the moss and explained that people's fathers made a living from selling the moss (which was true of a couple of families, though not of J. Wyddyn and Mr. Malone who both taught school in the winter). We said that the big kids had chased us out onto the rocks and fallen and hurt themselves. Which was true; after all, we didn't make them chase us, nobody twisted their arms. The big kids got in all kinds of trouble. They had to rake up the moss they'd scattered as a starter, and I don't know what all else. After that, though, it wasn't safe for us to use the causeway road because they were always laying for us. One of them lived near enough the road so it was hard to avoid him.

We took to using the dory, rowing around the point and going into the village that way. Sometimes we tied up by the main wharf, but after one of the kids caught Bobby coming off the wharf, we changed over to Mr. O'Brien's. The summer kids tried waiting for us there too, but only once. We yelled for help and Adonis came out and showed his teeth at them. After that we'd generally take Adonis with us for an escort, so everything worked out just fine.

Then after a series of slim catches, we shifted the traps over to the other side of the harbor. This had the advantage of being away from everybody else's fishing grounds so we didn't have to throw back the shorts because someone saw us so often. By this time rowing places had stopped being sheer fun and was beginning to look more like plain hard work, so we asked Joe if we could leave the dory in his yard. He gave us permission and we transported our two rollers for dragging it up and from then on left it beside his house. Joe always got on really well with kids. He didn't seem to feel about kids the way he did about adults. I suppose he had that romantic notion so many adults do that kids are sweet and pure of heart or something. Of course they aren't, any more than adults are, but it's a good thing adults think so. Otherwise you'd never get away with anything. It helps counteract the equally erroneous notion that other adults have that all children are wild animals, so it comes out even in the end.

Another advantage to the new place was that it was far more convenient to the harbor. There are wonderful big, fat flounders there; you catch them with rotten fish or clams, using a hook and line. Joe bought flounders too, and so did our parents and neighbors unless we had too long a run of luck and everybody got sick of them.

I like line-fishing because you catch something just about every time you let down your line. Cunners mostly, of course, which are trash fish, but it was fun to throw them to the gulls. There were always a couple of dozen of them waiting around to be fed; they catch the fish in the air before they hit the water. We gave a lot of flounders to Mr. O'Brien, sort of as rent for using his wharf. We tried to give them to Joe too, but he insisted on paying us fifty cents a fish.

After the Miss Finch episode we also began running errands for Joe. He acted as if he didn't like going into town, and after we started using his yard for the dory we used it to do just about all his shopping for him. He was always telling us to keep the change, but we wouldn't. We did agree that the deposit money on bottles was ours though, and did keep that.

We had about ten different routes from our homes to the breakwater. The longest was around by way of the rocks and had the disadvantage of crossing a section of the cobblestone beach, which is impossible to walk on because the stones roll underfoot and hurt your ankles. We could also go along the edge of the cliff, where there was a path, and there were various other combinations involving people's yards and the two flights of wooden steps that were built up the cliff. We didn't like the steps because they were too splintery for even our horny feet. If the summer kids were after us we went by the rocks because after their experience they weren't eager to go on them again, and even if they did, which they did a couple of times at high tide thinking they didn't have to worry on the rough-cut boulders like the ones in the breakwater that are dumped all the way round at the foot of the cliff, they still couldn't catch us, and they always ended up falling and getting hurt.

In most ways that summer was like any other summer. The days were long and hot, the evenings blue and cool. We spent an unbelievable amount of time doing just about nothing, popping tar-bubbles in the road with our toes (some are empty but some squirt hot water, and it's a challenge to see how long you can do it without getting tar on your feet), watching the creatures in the tide-pools at low tide on the rocks. There are pink crabs and two-tone green ones with designs in light on dark, there are minnows and clumps of horse mussels fastened to the rocks with hairy strings. We believed that horse mussels were deadly poison. I don't know if that's true or not. Gulls eat them. There are black snails all over the place and white snails with thick pointy shells on the house-rock (that's the very big rock near the low-tide mark). Never anywhere else, I don't know why. We used to catch hermit crabs and get them to fight by taking them out of their shells and putting them in a pool scooped out in the sand with only one shell between them (in a tide-pool they'd go hide under something and that was the end of that because you'd

88

never find them). The crabs would fight over the shell until one of them managed to get into it, then the other one would run off and sulk. We always gave the other one his shell back before we let them go. We'd also take a crab with too small a shell, find it a big enough empty one and try to guess how soon it would work up enough nerve to switch.

I used to take hermit crabs to Joe to watch, and he enjoyed them; he smiled as if he was actually enjoying himself. I took him regular crabs and minnows to watch sometimes too, in a jar, but he didn't seem to care for them much. He'd watch them long enough to be polite and then tell me to dump them back into the sea before they died.

One of the best things about summer was that we didn't have to be home before dark, and it was wonderful fun to go down to the village just before bedtime, in the coolness, and get a roll or bun cheap at the bakery just before it closed. The dory would seem to slide more easily than usual through the water, and there was a calmness to everything, a quietness so you could hear the oars splash and the water droplets pattering back into the water. Dusk is the best time of day, I think; everyone seems willing to stop a little and relax, and it's quieter than usual. I like to see the lights come on, and see the lighted-up ships far out near the horizon, looking as if they're floating in the sky because the horizon is too vague to make out.

Up until this year the Navy blimp used to fly in from patrol and slowly circle the harbor before going inland just about dusk. It said U.S. Navy on one side and Goodyear Tires on the other, and it made a quiet, satisfactory sort of noise with its propeller.

We'd go around the library and into the big alley behind the stores. The boys always wanted to check the trash behind Poe's Garage. They always hoped to find something as useful as the grill, and they found some pretty good things from time to time. The garage always smelled oily and often also of hot metal; the alley smelled of garbage and flowers, lilacs in May and roses the rest of the warm months. The bakery, of course, smelled of fresh bread and chocolate. The back door of the bakery had an electric fly-screen. We'd push it open cautiously, all of us having gotten a shock more than once, and go in through the big dim kitchen with its huge ovens, wide breadboards and shining stainless steel mixing bowls and utensils.

Mrs. Cellier, who owns and runs the bakery, was one of our favorite people; she still is for that matter. She always closes her shop at dusk in summer and sells whatever is left over for half-price. We'd go and buy buns, or whatever else she had, and if she wasn't busy with another customer, she'd butter the buns for us, or sometimes even put on her home-made quince jam, which tastes better than any jam anywhere. We'd take our buns or whatever we'd bought, and go to sit on the seawall to eat them before going home.

From the open windows of the Odd Fellows' Hall, which is over the butcher shop, would come the sound of the Mackerel Cove Brass Band. The band has one bass drum, three cornets, a piccolo, a Sousaphone, a saxophone, and a glockenspiel. They know three tunes: *God Bless America* which they play in unison very slowly and badly; the one that goes, "Oh the monkey wrapped his tail around the flagpole . . ." and the one that goes, "Be kind to your webfooted friends, for that duck may be somebody's mother. . . ." In these two, the piccolo plays the tune while the bass drum goes, "Boom boom, boom," and the Sousaphone goes "Oompah, oompah," and the glockenspiel, who is a non-conformist, comes in off-beat at odd moments. This throws everything off and, during rehearsals, everything comes to a halt while the bandmaster argues with the glockenspiel, who is penitent but does it again as soon as they get going.

We kids thought it was great fun but we were not unaware that the adults didn't share our enthusiasm. In fact, I think the Fourth of July is as big a deal as it is partly because the month of June is made hideous by their practising, and after the Fourth at least they go back to their usual schedule of once a month when they usually drink beer instead anyway.

Every two days during June a delegation of summer people turns up and complains bitterly about the band. For some strange reason the sound of it crosses the saltmarsh and arrives amplified at the rows of beach cottages between the marsh and the beach. This helps villagers to put up with it because, after all, it's the only band we have and we do take a certain amount of pride in it; at least we get miffed when it's criticized by outsiders. Mr. O'Connor makes it a practice to lower the rent five dollars in the middle of June, which keeps the summer people from rioting, or leaving.

The oddest thing of all is that, with all the practising, nobody ever seems to improve. The band has always sounded the same ever since I can remember. At Christmas they play *Silent Night* and *God Rest Ye Merry Gentlemen* in their best oompah style, but that's not so bad because they rehearse with the windows shut in winter. Besides, as my mother says, it's a real experience to hear *Silent Night* played on a piccolo with a bass drum and Sousaphone as accompaniment. And it is. In fact, you can hardly recognize it, though you keep feeling that the air is hauntingly familiar.

The band also plays at the Memorial Day parade, but it always rains so nobody turns up but the band, the Boy Scouts, and the relatives of the Band and Scouts.

7

Independence Day is the big thing in Mackerel Cove. We have a big parade with floats and everything. *Everybody* comes. Half the town's on parade and the other half watches, and of course all the summer people come to watch, and a few of them even get in it.

Fourth of July floats were a big deal. The only trouble was that the Beaver Patrol always won the grand prize. The Beaver Patrol lived inland and all in the same general area and their patrol didn't break up with the end of school the way all the others did.

We kids on the point didn't like Scouts a whole lot; we went because it's one of those things you sort of have to do, and no matter how good your reasons for not going are, the adults don't care. If you ask them why do you have to belong when it isn't that much fun they stop making sense and ask, "Don't you love Your Country?" Or something like that that has nothing to do with the case. So then you answer that of course you love your country and they say, "Well then, that's fine, run along to your meeting like a good girl." As if you'd agreed with them that you liked Girl Scouts, which you didn't at all.

There's no point talking to someone when they start thinking like that, and it doesn't make that much difference, so why argue? It's easier just to go along the way you're told and forget the whole thing. I mean, why make a federal case out of it?

Brock says I'm chicken because I'd rather agree than make a fuss, and he's always getting lumps because he stands there and tries to point out to people where they aren't being logical. All this ever has accomplished is to make the person in question raving mad, because nothing makes a person who is being illogical madder than to be told he is. You'd think Brock'd learn. As I told him, "You can't fight City Hall." On the other hand I sure admire him for having the backbone to stand up for his principles. I sort of wish I did, but not enough to do much about it.

But back to the floats; we always intended to outdo the Beaver Patrol and swore mighty swears the day after the Fourth that next year we really would, for sure, get organized in time, but by the time next June rolled around there were always a million other things to do, and you know how it is. It would be the first of July before we knew it and we'd have to run around like crazy-mad just to decorate Mr. Goodfellow's cart. Mr. Goodfellow lives on the point and has a cart and horse he always lets us use. The horse is an ex-milk-horse named Dandy. Dandy isn't as old as you'd think from the way he acts, he's just the most placid horse alive. When Mr. Goodfellow went all motorized a few years back he kept Dandy for old time's sake and be-

cause he'd gotten fond of him. We can ride Dandy bare-
back any time we want, and he'll plod around the pasture a couple of times out of sheer good will before he
sort of grinds to a slow stop and starts eating grass
again. Mr. Goodfellow keeps his cows and trucks and
things down near the cemetery, so his barn on the point
is empty except for Dandy and the cat. The cat sleeps
in the corner of Dandy's feed trough and even has
kittens there. She and Dandy are friends; horses are
funny that way. I wonder how Dandy keeps from eating a kitten by accident? Maybe he spits them out if he
picks one up by mistake, or maybe he's just a careful
eater. I should think a horse would feel about eating a
kitten the way I'd feel about eating a mouse by accident, or a bug. But then, I wouldn't let bugs or mice
nest in the corner of my plate.

Anyway, that first year Joe was there, when I was
eleven, it rained the first half of June so with nothing
else to do we remembered our vow to outdo the Beaver
Patrol. We wasted a week first-off arguing about what
to make and how to make it, and finally decided to
make a huge lobster out of papier-mâché and fasten it
to the wagon.

Dad gave us permission to build the lobster in our
garage and half of us were going to work on that while
the other half of us made a papier-mâché rock on the
wagon. We talked Bobby Wyddyn's and Oakley's older
brothers and sisters into helping us with the frame-
work, otherwise we'd never have been able to do it. We
used wood and chicken wire, then we made great slimy
pailsfull of flour paste and collected half the old news-
papers in town and covered the whole thing with
papier-mâché.

Then we smoothed it down and painted it. We got very perfectionistic about the paint job and even brought up live lobsters to copy. Then we varnished it, and it was beautiful. It was shiny as a wet lobster, olive green with black freckles and scarlet shadings at the edges, and fierce eyes. It was eight feet long, with ten-foot feelers and claws open and extended as if ready to bite. The feelers were the hardest part, they kept breaking.

The morning of the Fourth the boys, who had done most of the work on the wagon, hitched up Dandy and brought it over for us to attach the lobster. They'd made a big rough gray rock out of papier-mâché and they'd fastened big seaweed to it with carpet tacks. It looked magnificent but unfortunately there had been a three-day heat-wave and you could smell it coming a block away.

The older kids who'd helped us flipped and began running around spraying it with things to keep off the flies and tone down the smell and so forth, and in between tried to talk us into taking off the kelp. But the boys had spent days out in the dory fishing it up with an old moss-rake and they weren't about to take it off.

I got tired of listening to everybody argue and took my bike and went off to see Joe. There were still three hours to the parade, which started at one o'clock in front of the school.

I left my bike by the fence and ran over towards Joe when I saw him sitting out in his yard. I was talking a blue streak, all about the float and everything. He listened, I think with interest; he seemed interested. Then I asked him where he was going to be in the parade and he got mad. He didn't say anything, but I could tell from looking at him.

I goofed then; I started going on and on about how veterans in wheel chairs were all lined up on this big float I'd seen on TV. He interrupted me; he shouted, "Will you shut *up*?"

"What's the matter?" I asked, taken aback.

"If some idiots want to make spectacles of themselves —all right, but I'm not going to be in any damn parade, have you got that? There's nothing more disgusting than a cripple going around showing off what's the matter with him, like a stinking beggar shoving an ulcerated fist under your nose."

I was surprised and taken aback by the suddenness and intensity of his anger; he'd never shouted at me before. "Gee, I'm sorry. I never thought of it that way." I apologized, then when he seemed to have accepted my apology, I asked, "But you'll *go* to the parade won't you? You've just got to see our float."

"No, I will not go to your damn parade, and that's final."

He was still mad, but not as angry as before. My feelings were hurt and I guess I must have showed it because he began to look as if he was sorry. "Why not?" I asked, sniffling a little. He looked sorrier, so I added in a small, suffering voice, "Please don't be mad."

That was the first time I deliberately acted a little more hurt than I really was. I've never known if Joe saw through my act or not, but he always was gotten by it. "I'm not mad at you, Jessica," he said, real quick and apologetic. "But I won't go to your parade, and that's final."

"Not even to see our float?" I asked, still small and sad.

"I wouldn't go if the President of the Universe was there," he said. "If I go everybody and his brother will be pointing me out, 'There goes that crazy cripple that lives in the old Prescott place. I hear he's tetched in the head'."

"Nobody around here says 'tetched'," I informed him stiffly. I felt he was ridiculing me personally.

"Maybe not, but you get the point don't you?"

"I don't think people around here are that mean. They wouldn't say anything like that."

"But they'd think it."

"Well, if they did it'd be your fault," I said, losing my temper. "If you didn't go around laughing like a hyena in everybody's face, if you'd *let* somebody talk to you, maybe you'd find out people around here are just as nice as anybody."

He said a dirty word and turned his chair around real quick and began wheeling back toward the house.

"You're mean!" I yelled after him, "You're just plain poison-mean, that's what you are. . . . It wouldn't hurt you one little bit to just see our float, you're a nasty selfish old meanie." And I began to cry for real.

He turned around and came back. "Jessica," he said, real nice, "I'm sorry, but I can't go. Don't you see?"

"No, I don't see, I don't see at all,' I said, still bawling. I was awfully disappointed because all that time I'd been in the hot garage working away in the smell of Brock's mice, papier-mâché-ing and painting and varnishing, I'd been thinking how Joe would like the lobster. I'd wanted it to look good for him. But I couldn't explain that somehow. It wasn't that definite a thought back then, and besides I was hurt.

"I'll tell you what," he said, "I'll drive down and park by the causeway after lunch. You'll have to cross the causeway with it, and I'll see it then. All right?"

"All right," I agreed finally. Half is better than none, after all. I'd imagined him seeing it to the accompaniment of the band, and I'd imagined him saying how much better it was than the Beaver Patrol's; I'd imagined waving to him as we passed, but at least he'd see it.

"And then I'll drive back home and watch the parade with my field glasses," he added.

"All right," I agreed grudgingly. It still wasn't what I'd hoped but would have to do. I knew Joe wasn't going to change his mind.

To seal the bargain we went in and had a coke, and then I went home.

I just finished saying that I'd built my part of the lobster for Joe. That isn't exactly true. I built it also for my mother and father and the kids I was working with and myself. But in a sideways sort of way, deep down inside, I kept thinking of what Joe would think of it . . . he was the audience I had in mind, the only audience I cared very much about, so in a way it was for him. I couldn't possibly have explained that even to myself at the time. If somebody else had said I had I'd have told them they had rocks in their head.

I wonder why I cared so much what Joe thought? As I've said, I can't recall ever liking him an awful lot, but liking didn't have anything to do with how I felt about him.

Recently Brock had a short and tragic love affair (not full undress, only from the waist up) with Marshmallow (her real name is Marsha Mullens, but everybody calls her Marshmallow because she used to be fat and square, now she's all of a sudden got a 38-inch bust and everything). Brock said right along he didn't like her, he was in love with her. I asked him if it was all sex, and he said not entirely, that being in love was different from sex even though it was very much connected. He was actually quite vague, but I think he meant the difference between liking someone as a friend, somebody you can trust and all that, and being hung up with someone so you can't leave them alone, or stop thinking about them.

I wasn't that hung up with Joe, but I suppose in a baby sort of way I was in love with him, or my idea of him. After all he was a dragon-slayer and had the scars to prove it. Maybe being "in love" as distinguished from just plain loving is a matter of caring more for the idea of a person than for the person? I think so. I've never been really for-sure in love though; at least I don't think so. From what I've seen, being in love involves being miserable as well as hyped-up happy. And also seems to involve making a complete fool of yourself about once a day as an average. I don't think I want to be in love, it's too much work. But maybe you have to be in order to find out the difference between love and sex and liking.

Somehow I can't see myself falling head-over-heels stupid in love though. I'm too practical. I sure hope falling in love isn't necessary. There was this boy Ronnie that had a crush on me last year at school, and he was a good-looking clunk, and bright and all that, and I even kind of liked him, but try as I might I just couldn't seem to get a crush back. It made me feel mean. Here was this poor clod moaning around like a hound-dog with a belly ache and looking at me like I could cure him by giving him a puppy biscuit, and it made me want to laugh. I'm sorry, but I couldn't help it. I managed not to. Knowing Joe had taught me at least one thing, which is how much it can hurt to be laughed at when you feel you don't deserve it. But lunch with Ronnie just broke me up. He'd sit there across the cafeteria table from me with mayonnaise running down his chin (he always doused everything with mayonnaise) and gazing at me like a sick fish. I'd nearly bust a gut trying not to laugh in his face and I was forever choking on something from not laughing, and every time I choked he'd act like I'd contracted a fatal disease and run around like a chicken with its head cut off . . . which really undid me, and I'd have to make a mad dash for the girls' room to laugh before I really did choke to death.

> "When in doubt
> Scream and shout
> Jump up and down
> And run about."

Out of sheer guilt I used to go walking with him along the beach and sometimes when he forgot he was "in love" he wasn't half bad. He had an eye for things, like sandpipers and the color of the sea, and he knew a lot about books and about animals. But every so often, no matter how hard I tried to keep it clean, he'd feel the necessity to unburden his soul to me, and I felt so small and mean I couldn't stand it, because it's awful to have somebody try to give you everything when you can't return the compliment and don't want it in the first place. And it made me mad too, because it isn't fair to hand somebody your guts and leave them stuck with them so they have to carry them around like some kind of albatross.

Finally one day on the beach Ronnie confided in me that he "knew" I loved him because my going off to cry in the girls' room proved it, and all those lunches came floating up to mind, and the mayonnaise on his chin and the fat ham-and-tomato sandwiches held just below his fatuous grin . . . and this time there was no girls' room to run to, and I couldn't help myself. I just howled until I was so weak in the knees I had to sit down on a rock. Ronnie hasn't spoken to me since.

And I don't blame him a bit. It was a cruel thing to have done, even if I couldn't help myself. I wonder, stop to think of it, if Joe couldn't help laughing the way he did? My laughter must have sounded as cruel to Ronnie as Joe's did to me. And Joe had a lot more reasons than I did . . . he laughed to protect himself from pity, to keep himself from being laughed at. He was a proud man as well as a bitter one.

Anyhow, I tried to apologize and explain to Ronnie, but, of course, that only made it worse, because how on God's green earth could I explain? By that time he'd figured out what those muffled yelps coming from the girls' room *really* had been.

Ronnie nicknamed me the Snow Queen, and it stuck. So he got even because I hate that nickname. It not only means he thought I'm stuck up and cold, it also has a double meaning because he thinks that all that time I was just trying to be decent that I was leading him on, playing him for a sucker, in other words, giving him a snow-job. Which isn't fair at all.

One of the girls asked me why I didn't say nasty things back and I said, "It's not worth the effort." Which wasn't why. I think it was that I felt I owed Ronnie a little loyalty—after all, he had been in love with me, and I'd hurt him dreadfully. But I couldn't tell anyone that because then they'd say, "You don't owe him a thing, look at what he's saying about you. Don't be a sucker." I think you're a sucker if you don't act the way that makes you comfortable with yourself. Someone else thinking you're a sucker doesn't make you one. For instance, you can't steal something that's been freely given to you. But it was all too complicated to explain, so I didn't. And I hadn't given Ronnie a snow-job. But now most of the kids think I'm some sort of Mata Hari.

And as for the idea of being cold—well, I don't know if Ronnie was right or not. I guess I was cold with him, at least in comparison with the fire *he* had going. And I can't imagine falling in love, so does that mean I'm cold way down deep? Ronnie accused me of being frigid, but he doesn't know any more about that than I do, and that's not much. He was strictly a from-the-neck-up boy (he had trouble with God). As I said before, I liked Ronnie all right, so I probably would have let him go farther if he'd been so inclined. To be absolutely honest I will admit I do like to neck; it makes me feel all squishy inside and sort of nice. I sure am glad now though that Ronnie was afraid to do more than neck genteelly, especially after his nicknaming me and all that.

Brock said, "Let that be a warning to you. What if

you'd let him go farther and then broken up, think how you'd feel." *Let* him—that's a laugh.

I told Brock that maybe if Ronnie had the nerve to go farther I'd not have found him so excruciatingly funny. I mean, he'd have seemed more of a man to me. He also gave in too darn easily. Any whim—he'd do what I told him to. Like the time I told him to wade out and get me a hunk of driftwood I saw floating knee-deep in the water, just to see if he would. And the jerk did it. It was a nasty cold day with a raw wind, and the water was just about freezing, and the creep did it with hardly an argument. If he hadn't argued at all I'd have thought he was being gallant, but he argued just enough to spoil that. He should have told me to go fly a kite, that if I wanted a scummy old hunk of driftwood so darn much to go get it myself.

I guess, stop to think about it, I *was* pretty hung up with Joe St. George. Maybe you could even say I had a sort of crush on him—only not in the sappy way you think of crushes, because I didn't go around mooning over him or anything. In fact, I forgot about him for days at a time and that's not how crushes work. But I guess I do think of him when I go out with a boy, and sort of measure the boy against him. Which, I realize, isn't fair to the boy because Joe was, after all, a man, not a teenager. As a teenager he probably wasn't a bit better than the boys I go out with. But I can't help it; Joe's lodged there in the back of my mind and I can't help referring to him.

That Fourth of July was one of the few times Joe gave in to me, and even then he didn't give in all the way, he compromised. It was probably one of the kinder things he did, understanding that his seeing the lobster was very important to me and agreeing to go to some trouble to see it. But it wasn't giving in to a whim, it was being big enough to make a little kid happy. If he'd given in all the way and gone to the parade itself I probably wouldn't have respected him as much because going would have really gone against his grain.

I seem to have gotten pretty far from the float. Joe did wait by the causeway in his car, and did see it. Smelled it too, I guess, but he never mentioned it, which was another kind thing.

I guess it must have been pretty awful. But after working on it and everything we'd gotten used to it and stopped noticing it, and decided that the smell had "aired out." We drove grandly across the causeway, Dandy looking very elegant in a very slightly tattered ostrich plume donated by Mrs. Malone for the top of his bridle. The plume nodded regally and was, we all agreed, the finishing touch to a magnificent float.

We'd timed it so we'd be right on time, neither early nor late. We arrived in state, surrounded by a miasma of rotten sea-food, and we thought every head turned our direction because of our magnificence.

Then we saw the Beaver Patrol's effort and our hearts sank. It was an enormous papier-mâché eagle with a shield and mottoes. And it didn't smell. When I say we'd forgotten the smell that isn't quite true; I guess we knew it was pretty strong. But I know that not one of us realized exactly how terrific it was to an unaccustomed nose. We were put out when we were assigned the last place in the parade and felt we were being unfairly discriminated against.

But it was a marvel of a day, bright with sun with a fresh gusty breeze in off the ocean. You could see cats-paws of wind ruffling the water, and the sailboats would heel over as the wind passed over them filling their sails, and then straighten and scoot ahead with the acquired momentum.

The band started up, "Boom, boom, boom, oophah-pah," and about in front of the library the glockenspiel got really out of hand and went playing away at a great, wonderful, off-beat clip, and the piccolo doggedly pierced the ears with "Oh the monkey wrapped his tail around the flagpole . . ." and everybody got into the spirit of things and began marching instead of ambling along. Even Dandy was stepping with the drumbeat. Everybody in town who owns any kind of horse turns out on it for the Fourth and half the horses were plodding along looking bored and the other half, who didn't like the looks of the Beaver Patrol's eagle right behind them, were seesawing back and forth all wall-eyed and lathered, with red-faced sweating riders cussing them under their breaths.

Everybody who could beg, borrow, steal, or exhume from mothballs any kind of uniform was marching along in a sort of formation with their chests stuck out. We have everything from a fake Minuteman costume and a genuine Civil War Captain's uniform to a whole batch of World War One, Two, and Korean uniforms. In our town there are few Army uniforms, but many Navy and some Air Force, and most of them are World War One vintage. Why do men that age seem to like to march around more than anybody? Their uniforms are usually too tight and they're old enough to be silly but not old enough to be romantic or even quaint. Oh well, they like to, so why not? And they add to the fun because usually some of them have stopped at Patrick's

Pool Parlor for a beer or three and halfway to the Mackerel Cove Cemetery they start singing "When Johnny comes marching home again" in counterpoint to the band's webfooted friends.

We have a real, authentic Revolutionary soldier in our cemetery. He happens to be a Redcoat with an unpronounceable German name, but he's authentic, which is what counts. At any rate, there aren't that many Revolutionary soldiers around that you can afford to quibble about which side he was on.

The story is that a patrol of Redcoats came through scouting out the harbor, which hadn't silted up yet back then and could take fairly large ships. The Mackerel Cove militia ambushed them and shot three of them. Two were only lightly wounded and ran off, limping, with the others, but our soldier was mortally wounded and his companions left him for dead. When the Redcoats had gone the militia came over to him, and he said some things in German, but of course nobody understood him. Somebody sent for the schoolmaster, who knew some German, but by the time the schoolmaster got there the soldier was dead.

They buried him where he'd fallen and that was how the cemetery got started, because it was as good a place as any for one, and I think the people felt sorry they'd killed him. He was only nineteen, they found out from his papers, and his birthday was to have been the following Friday. There was a half finished letter to his family, asking about his fiancée and about the white plow horse.

He was just some poor slob of a Hessian who probably didn't have anything in particular against the colonists, but just wanted his pay to save so he could go home and get married. He must have felt terrible when he found himself dying in the inhospitable wilds of New England with an ocean between him and his home. I imagine him lying there in the sand and rain with a big wound in him somewhere and thinking, "Why did I ever sign up? My God, why?" And maybe dreaming about walking behind a plow in a straight furrow, and coming home at night astride a great fat German carthorse, the white horse named Freda that he asked after in his letter. I'm glad that they shoot a volley over his grave. I'm glad we make a fuss over him and bought him a new gravestone last year for five hundred dollars made of the best Vermont marble. It must be a terrible thing to die in a strange land where you don't even know the language and can't explain any last little thing to anyone.

Just landwards of the cemetery there's a ridge of ground; the road parallels it for a while, going between the cemetery wall and the fence of Mr. Goodfellow's cow pasture. It's always hot along that stretch because the ridge cuts off the breeze. We rode along that day watching the cows, who always watch the parade with a disapproving air, like old-maid schoolteachers. The music acquires more volume there too, and gets really into your blood. Because of the louder music and the lack of wind you always get the feeling that something important and special is about to happen, and somehow when you top the ridge you aren't quite disappointed because there below you lies all of the harbor and the big blue sea. But this particular year, something did happen.

Just as the Beaver Patrol's float topped the ridge, one of those little wind-squalls came by. The eagle was fastened on top of a jeep, and apparently somebody hadn't fastened it tight enough. We all said afterwards, "Just what you'd expect from a bunch of landlubbers."

Anyway, the wind caught the eagle and lifted it right up into the air and it went kiting off tail-first over the fence and into the cow pasture. The cows flipped and began running around with their tails in the air. They didn't give milk for a week. The horses, who had had their doubts from the beginning, went straight up into the air and ran off in seven different directions. The riders hadn't been watching the eagle as closely as the horses had and half of them were caught by surprise and ended up sitting in the road looking astonished. We sat on our seaweed and watched. Dandy looked walleyed at the eagle when it came over, decided it wasn't worth the effort of getting excited about and proceeded to go to sleep. Everybody else in sight ran around and shouted.

In due course the parade got going again and we wended our way to the cemetery. They fired the muskets over our soldier's grave, and some egg-head kid from sixth grade recited the Declaration of Independence in a whiny monotone, just like always. But all through the first half of the Declaration of Independence we could hear an unhorsed rider saying plaintively, "Nice horsie, here horsie, *nice* horsie." Nice horsie obviously wasn't having any, because somewhere around "He has refused for a long time" the voice said, "All right you crummy beast, go to hell." Which broke everybody up. Fortunately the boy-wonder reciting the thing lost his place and went blank so we were spared the rest of it. Do you have any idea how *long* the Declaration of Independence is? It's absolutely endless. And a lot of it I don't consider particularly edifying since it's mostly about what crumbs the British and George III were. Dad says it doesn't hurt anybody to hear it once a year, and I suppose he has a point, but gee-whiz, do they *have* to always have some little kid drone it out? If I was organizing it I'd get the best speaker in town to read it with feeling, then maybe it wouldn't put you into a coma.

Anyway, thanks to the mishap of the eagle and Dandy's placid personality we won the prize that year. Our lobster was a beauty (it just about killed us to have to throw it out) and the only other float that came up to it at all was the Beaver Patrol's. I think we really earned the prize. It wasn't our fault the kelp hadn't kept better; ordinarily it would have, and if it hadn't smelled so I'm sure we'd have gotten the prize even if the eagle hadn't taken off.

Afterwards Joe said he'd seen everything through his binoculars (which he called field glasses) and said that our lobster was by far the best, much better than the eagle. We told him about how the eagle scared the cows and horses (he'd seen the horses take off but hadn't seen the cows on account of the ridge) and about the person calling the horse, and Joe laughed. For once he sounded as if he was amused, and it was a nice laugh. He even said that he wished he'd gone, but in the subsequent years he didn't go, so I guess he was just saying that. Maybe he meant that he wished he'd gone that one year, maybe he meant it at the moment he said it. Probably.

8

That winter, after school started, I saw a lot less of Joe, naturally. Mondays was piano lessons, and I had to practise for half an hour every day. I have neither the talent nor the inclination for music and although I'd taken lessons since first grade I hadn't gotten very far. In November, when I told Dad all I wanted for my twelfth birthday was to be allowed to quit, Dad and Mom agreed that I could. It was the best birthday present I got.

Wednesdays was Scout meetings. I got kicked out three times and reinstated three times "on condition." The first time was for tickling Grace Mills during Artificial Respiration. The second was for punching tattletale Lydia Pennywhistle in the nose for telling Mrs. Sneed I had a novel in my Geography book. (It was the third time she'd done it and I'd *warned* her.) The third time wasn't entirely my fault. I'd been taking a mouse Brock gave me to school for weeks, and that day it crept out of my pocket and all the stupid girls had a fit. By this time Miss Banner was prepared to believe the worst and was positive I did it on purpose. When I told her indignantly that I was not the kind of girl who'd deliberately frighten a mouse (Goldie was absolutely terrified by all those big clumsy feet) she said I was being smart. After that I thought I was out for good, because I talked back and it got pretty sticky.

What happened was that she gave me the lecture about how Scouts was supposed to Build One's Character and stuff like that, and she said something to the effect that I should Love Scouts the way she did because it had done So Much for her. I couldn't help looking at her and thinking that if *that* was what it did for people I was well out of it (she's one of those big, square muscle-bound women with short hair and a man's suit, only with a skirt) and I guess it showed on my face because she really flipped. Honestly I didn't mean to let her see me thinking, it just happened. Then, of course, because she couldn't really say what I'd done to make her so darn mad, she had to make a bigger thing out of Goldie and tried to take her away from me. She was going to *kill* her. So you see, I *had* to bite Miss Banner, I didn't have any choice.

The gambit is that when you're kicked out of something compulsory (and Scouts is, no matter what they tell you) you're supposed to beg to be let back in after you've skipped one meeting. The first two times I'd done it because it was easier, and why make trouble for myself? Miss Banner taught Gym too, and that meant if she was down on a person, Gym was hell until she got over her peeve. But after what she said about Goldie I was determined not to beg to go back someplace I'd rather be anywhere than. I explained to Mom and Dad and they were very understanding about Goldie and all and said I didn't have to go back if I didn't want to. (Dad muttered something to Mom about not being able to stand women with hair on their chests himself. He thought I didn't hear him.)

The only trouble was that Miss Banner thought that her mission in life was to Build Character in everybody in sight and she couldn't stand letting me slip through her clutches. When I didn't beg to be readmitted to Scouts on schedule she cornered me in the locker room one afternoon and had a "talk" with me. The talk was bad enough, but I've always hated the smell of feet and stale people down there and I couldn't get out fast enough. Miss Banner was right in her element though; she'd inhale deeply as if the air was full of attar of roses. I didn't beg to go back to Scouts, although she led up to me doing so about ten times, and finally I escaped.

Then she started criticizing me in Gym until I felt like a freak with crooked legs three yards long and feet like a duck. It got so I was falling all over my own feet out of sheer nerves.

I told Joe about it one day. I stopped by his place on the way home from school. The last period of the day was Gym and I was still smarting from Miss Banner making me into a fool, otherwise I probably wouldn't have told anyone because just thinking about it made me ashamed. At the time I wasn't old enough to see that she was doing it deliberately; I kept thinking that I really was a clumsy ox, and as I said, I kept getting clumsier by the day.

Joe asked me what the things were I was having trouble with and I showed him. Miss Banner wasn't there with her eagle-eye to make me self-conscious, so I did everything well enough. Joe pointed that out and told me I was being clumsy in Gym on account of nerves and that I should know better. He then proceeded to drill me like a top-sergeant, and by the end of half an hour I had every move down pat. Then he told me a long complicated story about how certain soldiers get nervous and goof, and how one way to stop being nervous is to be really letter-perfect in what you're doing. By that time I was. Joe had a knack for explaining how to move, partly perhaps because he couldn't show you, and had to tell you. The next day Gym went off like a dream. I had my self-confidence back, and it was like I'd been oiled. Miss Banner couldn't find anything to criticize but my socks (they weren't pulled up). After that she didn't bother me a bit. About two weeks later she came to me and said that, considering that I'd Changed my Attitude, she had Reconsidered and was doing me the big, fat favor of allowing me to return to Scouts.

I almost told her I hadn't changed my attitude, but why make a fuss? I thanked her politely, even a little obsequiously, and she grinned like a rattrap with sheer delight. But I never went to another meeting; I'd *had* it. Of course she kept on my back, she didn't give up easily. Every week when I didn't show up she'd ask me the next day why not and I'd say eagerly that I'd come for *sure* next time, and she'd let it go until next week, etc. It was a comfortable enough arrangement and saved face all around. Brock accused me of being chicken, not to stand up to her and tell her how I really felt, but I still can't see what good that would have done. He said I shouldn't tell lies, and I suppose, theoretically, he's right enough, but gee-whiz, how are you going to get along with some crummy people if you don't tell them what they want to hear? They never hear you when you say something they don't want to hear, or else they turn what you said inside out so it comes out all backwards and different.

I talked to Joe about it, and he agreed with me. He said "You can't buck the system. The only thing to do is turn the handle the way it goes, only faster." And that is the best one-sentence-worth of practical advice anybody ever gave me. It works.

Every semester the different classes in school give Programs, which can be a lot of fun, only I always seemed to end up on the clean-up committee because I'm a hard worker and also because kids from the point tend to end up where nobody else wants to be. (It's our own fault for being so darn nautical all the time and calling everybody else landlubbers.) After Joe gave me that advice I tried turning the handle the way it goes. I volunteered for the decoration committee right off and was so shiny-eyed-eager that I got on it, so that then after, when the other kids tried to elect me to the clean-up committee, the teacher said I was already on the decoration committee and couldn't be on clean-up.

When I told Joe about it, he said to remember that the "only faster" part is important too, that if I didn't do a bang-up job on decorations I'd end up in clean-up again next time. So I did. I came up with a couple of good ideas and worked like a beaver, and incidentally had a ball. And next time all the kids said right off "Jessica for decorations."

I tried to explain to Brock, who was on clean-up then and thereafter, but he couldn't see the point. He's a prickly sort of person in some ways, because he's honest as a bone. It's not practical, but I admire him for it. I don't know if he really thinks bucking the system will eventually get somebody to pay attention to him, or if he just hopes so. If he ever did get an adult to really sit down and listen to him (I mean really listen not just say so and let it go in one ear and out the other) then I guess all the trouble would be worth it, because if an adult listened once to one kid he might try doing it again with other kids, and he'd find out that we're people too and that sometimes we have ideas that make sense.

I'm overstating it; what I mean is, not that nobody ever listens to kids, though some days it seems that way, but that much too often adults go around assuming things that just aren't true. (For example deciding that teenagers will have fun playing "The Witch is Dead" and bobbing for apples, and when we said we'd rather dance telling us we *ought* to enjoy little kid games.) I guess everybody does that though, not just adults. Though little kids don't as often, not the same kinds of things anyway, and when you tell them what's what, at least they'll listen to you before they tell you they don't believe you.

As I look back, that year I was in Sixth Grade (I was twelve in November) was a simple, easy year, and it seems as if the years before that were relatively simple too. It was after that next summer when Joe did the thing he did that everything suddenly got all complicated and different and difficult. I think I had more plain old-fashioned fun that school year than just about any year I can think of. Aside from the Scout thing, and that ended up just fine, everything went smooth as butter. There are times like that, when you can't do anything wrong, when even what looks like a goof seems to work out for the best. There are other times too, of course, when it's just the opposite, when you go around just brimming with good intentions and step all over your tail every time you turn around. Like last year. The Ronnie thing was the least of my troubles. They said I had the wrong attitude and didn't "co-operate" (whatever *that* is supposed to mean. They've never explained what they mean by it . . . what it effectively means is not to talk back, to act pleased about doing things you don't want to, and not to look at them with your thoughts showing.)

And it seemed as if I got blamed for just about everything that went wrong, from gum in the coin-return of the hall telephone (it's a clever idea, but it never would have occurred to me) to organizing the fuss over the cafteria's hot lunch stew (which I didn't eat because I brought lunch from home and only bought the soup and hot chocolate, which was fit to eat). Some kids had a song to the tune of "The Old Gray Mare" that they'd learned at summer camp, and every time the stew was served they'd start it up and we'd all sing it real loud. "Great gray gobs of greasy, grimy gopher guts, itty bitty birdie feet, petrified monkey meat. . . ." I think the words "gray" and "greasy" were what struck a nerve, because the meat in the stew was.

School work went differently after sixth grade too. Up until then it was easy and sometimes a little boring because it was a drag to have to sit there and wait for the dummies to finish things, but when we were supposed to be working I could pay attention. After the thing Joe did though, it got difficult to keep my mind on things and I'd find myself staring out the window daydreaming halfway through something instead of waiting until I was finished and then thinking about something. Dad was in an uproar because my grades had slipped, but Mom said it was normal for girls my age to be preoccupied. I wish it had just been my age; I'd have had some guarantee I'd outgrow it.

But all this hasn't much to do with what I was going to say about Joe, so I'd better stick to my knitting and get back to it. I asked Joe for a bottled ship for my birthday, but he wouldn't give it to me. In fact, I kept nagging him for a ship, and even saved up the money and begged him to sell me one for what Mrs. Root paid him, but he wouldn't sell it to me.

I asked for one for Christmas and he said "No." I whined and nagged, and begged and pleaded. I was winsome and charming for days on end. I didn't give the poor man a minute's peace. He said "NO!" Looking back on it, I wonder why he put up with me; I must have made myself thoroughly obnoxious.

Finally it penetrated my dense little skull that Joe meant it. That the "no" was final and that he couldn't be worked around in any way I know of. I suppose, if I'd put the same amount of pressure on my mother or father, they would have helped me earn enough to buy one from Mrs. Root, but I didn't want one from Mrs. Root. By the time she had bought it and was reselling it, it was something from the Lobster Pot, not something of Joe's. It wasn't the same thing at all.

Once I finally got the message that Joe wouldn't let me beg, borrow, or steal (as a matter of fact, that last never occurred to me. If it had, I wonder what I would have done?) a bottled ship, then I began to wonder why. So one day I asked.

It was a gray snowy day. Snow was falling softly and steadily, endlessly, disappearing into the sea and piling up fraction by fraction on land. Joe was rigging one of his miniature ships and talking about Yankee clippers. He had completed the hull, which he made with precision and put into the bottle piece by piece and glued together so when it was complete it looked like a single piece. He had a very small lathe for turning out the tiny brass cannons and cleats and so forth, and for turning wooden spars and other symmetrical pieces. He hand-carved most of the hull. I was holding the bottle with the completed hull. The name *Lucy* was lettered on it, it was a schooner and was going to be a two-master, and had a figurehead of a woman beautifully carved and painted. Joe was laying out the rigging and spars on a board in front of him, using tweezers because the elements were so tiny and hard to pick up by hand. It always amazed me, no matter how often and long I watched, to see a man of his size be so deft with such tiny splinters of wood. And always, his hands were absolutely steady, steadier than mine even.

The rigging is the hardest part, it's all done outside the bottle, put in, and then one line is pulled and it opens up like magic, everything in place. The long line that's used to pull it open is fastened to the bowsprit with a spot of glue and cut.

That day Joe was talking about the *Flying Cloud*. She was built by Donald McKay of Boston (who built most of the record-breaking clippers) in 1851. She was 1,783 tons, 225 feet long, 40 feet, 8 inches in the beam, and her mainmast from step to truck was 200 feet. She carried about two acres of canvas, with three standing skysails above her royals. Her master was Captain

Cressy, and Mrs. Cressy was her navigator and always sailed with her. Mrs. Cressy could reckon position using five-place logarithms from Bowditch. The *Flying Cloud* sailed from New York to Frisco, around the Horn, in eighty-nine days, twenty-one hours which is a record, and in 1852 she sailed 374 nautical miles in one day on a return voyage to New York. Her owners were so impressed they displayed her topmast fids at the Astor to show how they'd been splintered and broomed by the strain. In 1855 on the way home from China she hit a coral reef and nearly sank, but they managed to get her off and repair the hole in her hull at sea by shifting cargo. Her figurehead was a winged angel with a golden trumpet.

I liked the *Flying Cloud* best but there were many others Joe talked about. There was the *Sea Witch* under Bully Waterman who was almost lynched once for killing sailors during a voyage. She had a black Chinese dragon for a figurehead and once made the run from New York to Frisco in ninety-seven days. There was the *Sovereign of the Seas* with a figurehead of Neptune. She was almost totally dismasted on her maiden voyage, but although he was told it was impossible, the master saved all the rigging and re-rigged at sea during the same storm that had dismasted her and came into Frisco as good as new in 103 days, and that was the record for that month. In 1850 the *Oriental* made it from China to London in ninety-seven days and put all of London in a flap—they hardly believed it, but had to when they saw her lines.

In 1851 the *Stag Hound,* built in sixty days, made $80,000 profit for her owners on her maiden voyage to California and China. There was the *Rainbow,* the first true full-rigged clipper, built by Griffiths, who designed her. She ended up in the opium trade. And the *Houqua, Northern Light, Comet, Witch of the Waves, John Stewert, Swordfish, Ino, Lightening, Champion of the Seas* . . .to name a few.

All of them were record-breakers. They had short lives though, because they were made of soft woods and they had to be driven to the limit to make the profits required by their owners. They were as flat-bottomed as they could be made, short of capsizing, and drew as an average about sixteen feet of water, fully loaded. Their performance was so startling that it was said that the captains left port under full sail and padlocked the running rigging blocks to keep anyone from shortening sail. This is, according to Joe, simply impossible, but what they did do was incredible enough. These were ships designed to give top performance in heavy wind and they did poorly in light air. The masters took out totally untested ships, fresh off the ways, and ran them around the Horn under two acres of canvas. One reason they broke records every time they turned around was that, before the clippers, thirteen and a half knots was top speed for any ship and eight knots was average top speed for most.

I remember one time I mentioned a TV program where this man was complaining because he said Americans are speed-crazy. Joe said they always have been, and that if they weren't clippers would never have been built. And they were the first real innovation and improvement in ships since the Romans. They were great, marvelous ships and have never been equalled. If I mention them with enthusiasm, it's because I learned it from Joe.

He didn't just talk about clippers, he talked about the Atlantic packets, whaling ships, and other trading ships. He talked about schooners, brigs, hermaphrodite brigs (so-called because they were both square-rigged and fore-and-aft rigged) and so forth. But he liked clippers best and his enthusiasm about them infected anyone who listened to him.

But once I'd begun to wonder why he wouldn't give me a bottled ship, I also noticed that he never talked about the ships he constructed with such care and delicacy. So I asked him about the *Lucy*.

"She was constructed in 1797 in Norwich, Connecticut," he said, his tone unusually sober for him under the circumstances, because he always had a lot of life in his voice when talking about ships. Nor did he go on about her, which was unusual, because usually asking one question would set him going for at least a quarter of an hour.

"Tell me about her," I asked, when I realized he needed prodding.

"She sailed out of Bristol, Rhode Island; her master was a man named Charles Collins, a brother-in-law of a Charles DeWolf, who owned her. In 1799 she was condemned by the Providence District Court to be sold for the benefit of the government, but the owner pulled a fast one and bought her back for a pittance. She was a slaver."

By that time I'd listened to him enough and looked at enough pictures, to know a few of the finer points of sailing ships. I looked at the hull and then over at the rigging which was almost completed, and said, "She's beautiful. She looks fast."

"A slaver had to be," Joe said bitterly. "Running

slaves was illegal, and a slaver had to outrun just about every navy in the world."

"What happened if they didn't?"

"The ship that caught a slaver had her as a prize and could sell her. But in 1857 the *Wanderer* was caught by a British cruiser, and the master simply invited the officers to dinner, and they let him off scot free."

"Maybe they didn't know it was a slaver?"

Joe snorted. "It's said that a slaver could be smelled five miles away downwind. It's not likely they didn't notice a stench like that. It's also said that the slaves shackled below-decks moaned constantly, so some men on slavers ended by committing suicide, unable to bear it. Not many though; they were an iron-hearted crew. Ideal lading was 16 inches by 5 feet, 6 inches by 2 feet, 10 inches per head, and tween-decks was never more than six feet high, so once the slave-deck was in, that left three feet of headroom for each layer. The slaves were fastened in leg irons riveted to the deck, and the expected mortality was twenty per cent." Joe wheeled his chair back and around, marking out the size of the rectangle of space allowed, and it was hard to believe. I'll never forget those figures. "The slaves were packed so tight they had to lie down front-to-back spoon-fashion and they were crammed so tight and left so long that sometimes they left strips of skin on the planking when they were taken on deck for food and air. This was on humane slavers, mind you; I'm describing what was considered good treatment. When they aired the slaves they put irons on their wrists and chained them together and the crew went below to swab out the deck. It's said that even the most hardened slavers' crews retched at the stench, because there was no sanitation whatsoever, and the slaves weren't unshackled for twenty-four hours at a stretch. On the best of voyages, on the most humane of slavers, mortality was ten per cent. Sometimes the ships were caught in the doldrums and the whole cargo died. Some masters overcrowded their ships and more than half died. When the U.S.S. *Mohican* captured the *Erie* off the Congo River in 1861 there were 987 slaves aboard. The *Mohican* took the ship directly into Monrovia, but 600 had died before they could be unloaded. Some slavers, about to be caught, jettisoned the entire cargo, chained to an anchor. When smallpox or ophthalmia broke out, the cargo was jettisoned. That happened on the *Rodeur,* a French brig . . . but it didn't do the crew any good; a passing ship found her adrift in the Sargasso Sea with every man aboard blind." This isn't exactly verbatim; Joe said a lot more, but I've put down some of the facts I happen to remember. He mentioned a lot of other ships and many other incidents; he had it all in detail, just the way he could describe in detail the passages of the Yankee clippers that beat around the Horn and to China for tea. Anyway, this much will give you the idea.

I was horrified but somehow not deeply touched. So great a horror is too much to grasp, too immense to understand. It's far easier to write off the fact that a million men have died in a war than it is to accept the death of one single man before your eyes. It wasn't that I didn't believe Joe. I did. I'd checked some of his facts before, and he was never wrong. If he said a thing had happened in 1799, that was when it had happened. If he said the master of the slaver *Charlotte* was Captain Sabens, then he was. I agreed that it was all true and all dreadful beyond words, but it was too big and too far away in space and time. It didn't touch me. There was no human interest. If he'd told me a heart-rending story of one single poor man, then I could have wept for that man, but it's impossible to weep for ten thousand men in a bunch, because they have no faces.

I was more impressed by the amount of space Joe delineated on the floor than by anything else. I folded the scatter rug in my room to that size, measuring it as I went, and tried staying on it comfortably, and some very faint echo of a slave's anguish came home to me, but I was alone, unshackled, in a clean well-lighted room and I knew it. My experiment wasn't the same thing at all.

Joe talked for a long time about slavers, once he got started, piling fact on fact, name on name, date on date. I sat crosslegged on my cushion on the table watching the snow disappear into the gray sea and listened. At the end he said, "Now do you understand why I won't give you a ship in a bottle?"

I thought about it and said, "Yes, but I don't understand why you put them in in the first place." It wasn't hard to understand why he didn't want to give someone he liked, something evil in a bottle, but I couldn't understand why he wanted to make ships with evil reputations. "Why don't you put the *Flying Cloud* in a bottle and let me have it?" I wasn't nagging for a change, I really wanted to know why.

"Because I don't want to put the *Flying Cloud* in a bottle, that's why. She was a good ship."

"Why not make her and not put her in a bottle?"

"Jessica, you are persistent, aren't you? Do you want one of my ships that much?"

I nodded.

"Listen then, I'll tell you why not. Are you listening?"

I nodded, I certainly was listening.

"Promise not to laugh?"

"Why should I laugh?" I asked, puzzled. That was a funny thing for an adult to say, I thought.

"Promise first."

"Cross my heart and hope to eat a toad."

"O.K. Let's put it this way; it's a sort of game I'm playing with myself. A sort of race against time and death. I've decided that before I die I want to put a model of every American ship that ever was outstandingly evil into a bottle. Slavers and pirates. I try to get them exactly right, but if there's not enough information I fill in the details by guessing how they must have been rigged for their time and tonnage. You see?"

I nodded.

"There were hundreds of them and even the best was very evil. . . . There are so many of them, and I haven't much time. I could die tomorrow; even with luck I won't live long . . . five more years perhaps, ten at the outside. So you see, I haven't time to make you a clipper and not put it in a bottle, though I would like to."

"I see," I said solemnly, "Thank you." There was a current of understanding between us that afternoon; I knew that for this span of time I could trust him not to start laughing at me, or say he was teasing to throw me off the scent. Several days later he teasingly said that thing about corking up crumbs of the world's evil, but that afternoon he was dead-serious, and even if I couldn't have put what he meant into words, I felt what he meant, and understood.

Now I wonder why I didn't ask why he didn't in-

clude opium clippers in his category of evil ships. I
wish I had because. . . . No, if he'd decided they were
evil he wouldn't have given me one. I suppose he didn't
include them because he had to draw the line somewhere; if he'd lived longer and run out of pirates and
slavers he might have added them to his list.

It took him about a month to complete a ship, from
start to finish, though he generally had two or three in
various stages. When he got tired of the finicky work of
rigging he'd stop and turn some pieces of wood or metal
on the lathe, or do some carving on a hull, and so on.
In summer he made fewer than in winter because he
spent so much time outdoors in the sun.

That afternoon after I said "Thank you" he nodded
seriously and then there was a silence. He was busy rigging the schooner and I alternately watched him and
looked out at the snow. There's something hypnotic
about snow falling into water. After a while Joe began
talking about the Atlantic packets and the afternoon
became like any other, until just before I left.

Dusk was settling down fast even though the snow
had let up, and the road wasn't plowed yet so I was
going to have a weary trudge home. Joe saw me to the
door, as he always did, but just before I let myself out,
he stopped me by putting his hand on my arm. I looked
up at him, surprised by the break in routine.

He had a funny, sort of sad expression on his face.
"You're a good kid, Jessica," he said. "Listen, I want to
make you a very iffy promise. If I finish my evil ships,
or if I know I'm definitely not going to be able to
finish, then I'll make you your clipper. Which one do
you want?"

"The *Flying Cloud*," I said promptly.

"O.K. It's a deal. But the chances are you won't get it."

"I know it," I said. And I did know it. They say, "It's the thought that counts." Well, it is. I was happy because I knew Joe meant it, that he would if he could. It wasn't that he could but wouldn't as I'd thought before.

9

That winter went along like most winters, a few Northeasters and blizzards when school was closed for a couple of days. Christmas vacation and New Year's Eve at home when we were allowed to stay up till midnight. The days were short and cold, the sun very far away, a light in the sky with no substance or heat to its rays. Mostly the skies were gray and the ocean heaved sullenly beneath the clouds, a dull gray-green like slate. Sometimes in a sub-zero frost it was very clear and cold, and the stars were almost close enough to touch and the sea seemed even bigger than usual, and if you went outside the cold pinched your nostrils.

Brock spent a lot of time worrying over his mice and nagging to have them brought inside from the garage, but they didn't seem to mind, and no more than usual died. I think *he* didn't like the draught along the floor and the freezing walk back and forth before breakfast. Mom said Brock and I could invite Joe for Christmas, but he refused. I think because he disliked so having anyone help him, and someone would have had to take him up the steps into our house.

Mom and I drove down Christmas day with hot turkey and all the trimmings and found him sitting alone by his workbench with an uneaten ham sandwich. He was polite but distant and I found myself ill-at-ease because I had wanted him and Mom to like each other, and it seemed then as if they didn't.

On the way home Mom said she liked him though, so maybe I saw things wrong. She also was impressed by the absence of chairs. I'd gotten so used to sitting on top of the tables I'd stopped noticing.

Later, when Joe returned the dishes, he told me to thank her again for him and said she was a fine woman or words to that effect. He'd driven up in his car, and it was freezing cold out so our conversation didn't last long. He also said she was a looker for someone with two kids our age, and I didn't know if I should be mad at him or take it as a compliment. I passed it on to Mom, who said she was very complimented, then asked me what I was staring at. I guess I'd been staring because that was the first time I had really noticed that my mother was more than just "Mom," that she was a person who could be good or bad looking, that she might even be a stranger to someone. My mother is good looking, she's not fat and she's not stringy, and everybody says she has a wonderful smile.

That year, as always, spring was too slow in coming. The sunshine began to get some weight behind it but the wind still cut like a knife. April was a squally mess; it must have rained nearly every day. I hate gray days because the whole world seems so gray and hopeless. The sea always seems to amplify the mood of the sky, and when it's overcast, the water is sullen and cold, the color of a dirty sidewalk.

There is a window only an inch or so above floor level at the lower landing of the front stairs. That year I acquired the habit of taking a pillow and sitting there to read because I could look out the window and see the field next to the house instead of the ocean. Grass likes rain, and you can sit and think about all the greenness unfolding upwards and the hairy white roots probing downwards, and then it's not as depressing. That's about the only window in the house you can't see the ocean from, and as a matter of fact, facing the other way you can see it from that window.

Halfway through May the weather suddenly got nice. It was so warm I even went sunbathing in the back yard where the breeze couldn't nip me. The sky was high and dark blue and the sea looked happy, it sparkled and danced. It stayed that way for more than two weeks and all the daffodils and narcissi (we didn't have a duck that year so our yard was full of flowers) bloomed. Then it got cold and nasty again, and it rained some more. I was so mad when I woke up one morning and saw the sky that I kicked a chair and hurt my toe. Then after two days is cleared, much to my surprise, and the sky was full of long, thin, white streamers of cloud.

I came home from school at three and found Mom out in the yard beside the house looking at the sky. When she saw me, she asked, "Did you notice when the gulls began to fly inland?"

I shook my head, I'd been in school and hadn't had a chance to watch gulls. I looked around, and saw that there were very few gulls in sight and that they were uneasy. As I watched, a group of them rose up and flew inland crying plaintively to each other as they went. Below us, the surf was somewhat heavier than it should have been for the amount of wind we'd been having, and it seemed slower.

"I didn't either," she said, "I was cleaning upstairs."

"Let's go turn on the radio," I suggested.

"Small craft warnings are out,' she said. "But the glass is dropping and I feel as if it's going to be a bad one."

We went in together and looked at the old ship's barometer on the living-room wall. "Two millibars in the past hour," Mom said. "I'm going to call your father."

She asked Dad what he thought, and they had a long discussion about the gulls, the barometer, the waves and the clouds. Dad said he'd go ask Captain O'Brien, Antoine's father. The Captain is the local weather authority. Half an hour later the phone rang and Dad said that the Captain said it was going to be a bad one, and that Antoine and the O'Brien boys were working like beavers lashing down everything in sight. Mom gave Dad a list of groceries, and listening, I began to feel excited. She had candles, kerosene and hotdogs on the list, among other things, and that meant that she expected the electricity to go off.

By the time Dad got home at five with the supplies, the radio was issuing gale warnings. There was still no wind, but the seas were heavier, the combers slower and more ponderous, and the tide hadn't gone out as far as it should have. We went out after supper to look at things and the light was very strange and sinister, a sort of sickly green. The sea looked almost luminous, and was a shade of blue-green I've never seen it before or since, very dark and bright. It looked poisonous. There wasn't a seabird in sight, even the sandpipers were gone. A bunch of landlubber robins and jays were flying around the yard though, and convinced as I was by then that something big was about to blow up, I wanted to shout to them to fly inland. I said so to Brock and he and I tried to chase them away, but of course they didn't fly inland the way we'd hoped, but further out onto the point instead.

By the time we'd finished chasing the birds we were on the other side of the hill looking down at the harbor. Captain O'Brien had run up his own personal weather flags. He has this steel flagpole in front of his house and his greatest pleasure is second-guessing the weather reports and running up his flag indicating the weather before the radio says what's going to happen. He's usually right. This time he'd run up two square flags, which is the hurricane warning. We ran all the way home to tell Dad and Mom. By then we were almost popping with excitement. By this time the glass was dropping so fast you could almost see it, but still no wind and the sky was clear except for those long high-flying streamers of cloud which were heading right towards us. The radio was now mentioning a whole gale with winds up to 60 knots, but not a word about winds of hurricane force.

Dad mumbled something about "better safe than sorry," and got out the storm shutters for the two picture windows in the living room. He put them up and told Brock and me to be sure we hadn't left anything outside, like bikes.

Brock was flipped over his mice, and finally Dad and Mom talked it over and said he could bring them in and put them in the cellar. Dad helped Brock move the table he keeps the cages on, but Mom made Brock wash the table off with strong detergent before she'd let him bring it into the house.

We took another long look outside before Mom and Dad made us go to bed. It was still calm, and in the dark there was nothing to see. It was overcast by then though, because there were no stars. The bell buoy was tolling, it seemed to us portentously, in the harbor mouth, and the waves were crashing more heavily than before.

The storm broke sometime after midnight, shaking the house and waking us. Mom came in to close my windows, and I called to her, She said, "Wait a minute," and I heard her closing the other windows, then she came back. "What is it Jessica?"

"Is it really a hurricane?"

"If it isn't it's as good as one. At eleven the radio was predicting winds of hurricane force."

"Do you think Joe will be all right?"

"Why not? That house stood firm through a hundred storms as bad as this, why not this one?"

"I just wondered."

The next morning the glass was still falling. I'd hardly ever seen it so low. The wind was shaking the house and bellowing. On the seaward windows that weren't shuttered we could see little pieces of seaweed being deposited by the wind until we couldn't see out. Some were almost an inch square and, plastered flat on the glass as they were, you could see that some were green and others red. A hurricane force wind has a sound to it like no other wind on earth, a kind of harping, singing scream that is so loud it is also like the bellowing of some unbelievable beast.

Of course Dad stayed home, nobody could go out on a day like that, and we knew that the causeway would be underwater and probably Prescott Road as well. It doesn't take much of a storm to do that. Around noon a cat turned up at our back door. Heavens knows how it got to our house in all that wind and water, but it did and Mom heard it somehow and let it in. It proceeded to have accidents all over the house but Mom refused to put it out into the storm.

Brock's mice were nervous, either from the storm or the strange quarters, I don't know which, but Brock fed them, made sure the cellar door was tight to keep the cat out, and forgot them.

Besides his regular sales of 100 mice a month to the lab, Brock sells some to pet shops in November and December. (The demand for pet mice is very seasonal.) Brock had made a lot of money that winter but he hadn't bothered adding it up at the time so his books were in a hairy mess. We thought he could work Dad around to helping him, but Dad said Brock would have to get as much done on his own as he could first, and then he'd get help if he needed it. Then Dad settled down with a lapful of professional journals. This put Brock in a foul mood and also made him stubborn, so he ended up getting his books straight all by himself, but it took him all day long to do it.

Around noon I tried to phone Joe, but the telephone lines were already down, so I couldn't get him. Right after supper was cooked (which was lucky because we have an electric stove; it's too expensive to lay gas lines out to the point) the electricity went off. Mom had had the kerosene lamps ready since the night before, so we lit those and had candles on the table, and it was more fun than anything.

The eye of the storm came around ten o'clock the next morning and we all ventured out for a breath of air and to see the damage. The garage door had come unlatched and had pounded itself into splinters. Dad said we were lucky that was all and added a bit sourly that maybe the storm would air out the garage. He wanted Mom to put the stray cat out, but she refused. She said that the calm wouldn't last more than half an hour, if that, and that she wasn't going to kill the cat. There was quite an argument, which the cat solved by snaking out between Mom's legs and taking off. I don't know what happened to it, I never saw it again, but I didn't see its corpse either, so it may well have made it to some haven.

The calm lasted about fifteen minutes and then the wind was back, this time coming from the opposite quarter. By the next day I was beginning to get bored with the storm, and tired of the noise of the wind, which was so loud and insistent that you never could quite ignore it. We were running out of hot water; the tank is quite large but, without electricity to heat it, it was beginning to get lukewarm. I complained to Mom. I was trying out religion that year, and I told her that I'd prayed for the storm to go away and I was mad because nothing had happened. She said, "The trouble with most of us is that we can never remember to pray for patience instead of for the bus to come."

I got the message, and being a little ashamed of myself, countered by saying I was worried about Joe.

Then having said I was, I began to worry for real. The Prescott place is on a rise of ground but it's awfully near the water, and when we'd gone out during the calm we'd seen how heavy the seas were. The bell buoy had been going out of its mind, and the combers breaking on the beach were at least ten feet high. I also worried what would happen to Joe if he got sick and couldn't phone the doctor.

The next day the storm was gone and we all trooped out into the sunshine to see what it had done. The garage door was a total loss and after the wind had shifted, the trellis around the back yard had gone down, but aside from that and some badly salt-burned bushes, we were in good shape. The Wyddyns had lost a dory and the Malones had a cellar-full of sea water, Mr. Goodfellow's barn had lost a lot of shingles, but aside from that our neighbors were all right too. A lot of trees had been uprooted, which is what had brought the power lines down, but already the linemen were out repairing the wires.

I took off on foot for the breakwater; there was a tree down across the road by the Goodfellow place, so I knew a bike would probably be more trouble than it was worth. There were three more trees to climb over on the way to Joe's and all the trees standing were badly salt-burned. The leaves came out all curled and queer that year, except for the oaks which weren't far enough into leaf to be hurt.

I found Joe out in his yard hosing seaweed off his windows and looking happy. The surf on the breakwater was so loud we had to shout. When Joe saw me he asked, "How did you folks make out?"

"Fine," I yelled. "Neighbors are O.K. too. How about you?"

"Cellar's full of sea water."

When he called my attention to it I noticed the sug-sug of a pump going. "I was worried about you," I told him.

"It sure was some storm," Joe said happily, "but you shouldn't have worried; this house is made right. It's probably seaworthy, if it came to that."

That was the first time it was clear to me how much Joe loved that house. It makes sense, considering that it was built by a shipwright, and knowing how Joe felt about wooden ships.

Although the point got off lightly, partly because we were prepared and partly because the houses out here are built for weather, the town took a beating. Most of the stores on the main street were flooded when the seas slopped over the sea wall, and a number of windows were broken. The summer cottages between the beach and the salt marsh were all flooded and the front row had taken a real beating. One of them had a small sailboat jammed through its front door, and J. Wyddyn found his dory on the front porch of another. The dory was in better shape than the porch. Mr. O'Connor, who is also an insurance broker, was running around like a chicken with its head cut off assessing damage.

Then we heard that the sea wall by the cemetery had been breached and that the graves had been washed out. The boys wanted to go find a skull. We started down to the causeway and as we came over the hill saw that it was still underwater. We couldn't wait for the tide to turn, so we decided to take our dory and go by sea.

We knew perfectly well that if we had asked if we could go we'd get a flat "No." So we didn't ask. The seas were still very heavy and the breakers were running about six feet high but we figured we could get the dory launched by timing it to get past the line where they were cresting in between big ones.

First of all we went over towards the beach cottages to see where everybody was. All the men were over by the last row of cottages near the salt marsh. They were helping Mr. O'Connor nail sprung doors shut and board up windows and we figured that they'd be busy for at least another hour. We went back along the beach checking flotsam as we went, partly so it would look as if that was what we were doing there and partly because we didn't want to miss anything particularly good. By the time we got back near where the dory was we decided we were safe because we hadn't seen hide nor hair of any parents. We got the dory and dragged it down the beach on rollers, working as fast as we could so we would be out to sea before anyone saw us and showed up to stop us. We figured that once we were past the line of breakers we could say we were afraid to come back in and at least be allowed to take the dory into the quieter water at the harbor.

When we'd talked about timing the waves and getting off in between, it had sounded very simple, but when we got down to the water's edge they suddenly seemed to be coming much faster than we'd thought, and we were struggling with the dory and wet to the eyes when suddenly Oakley said, "Oh-oh!" and we saw a flying wedge of angry fathers bearing down on us from the direction of the beach cottages. Instead of giving up we all heaved and the dory went shooting out on top of the foam of the last wave. We jumped in and grabbed the oars and were just pulling away and clear before the next one crested when J. Wyddyn took a flying leap and grabbed the rope hanging from the stern.

Then everything happened at once: the water sucked out from under us, dropping us on the sand, and I looked up. The gray-green water was curving up and up big as a mountain. It thinned and hesitated as combers do just before they crash, and the sun's blur became a clear disc seen through the thin layer of water. The knife-edge crest thickened, the water behind it thinned, and over it came, gathering foam, like the walls of Jericho right on top of us. At the last moment I tried to dive up through the water, but I was encumbered by my boots and heavy clothes and there I was, not knowing which way was up, being tumbled around with everybody else in a smother of sandy water. Just before we all drowned the sea deposited us on the beach and withdrew. All the fathers were as wet as we were and J. Wyddyn's favorite cap was drifting out to sea.

Dad pulled Brock and me away from the water before the next one caught us, cuffed us both, and began swearing a blue streak. J. Wyddyn and Mr. Malone did the same with Oakley and Bobby. All of them were hopping mad and although we kids didn't learn any new swearwords (there aren't that many of them after all), we sure learned a dozen and a half new combinations. We'd probably all have been whaled on the spot, but somebody noticed that the dory was slipping deeper into the water. Our fathers dropped us to haul the dory in, then sort out of habit, dumped the water out of it and began hauling it up the beach. Then they noticed us again and made us haul it up the rest of the way, telling us what a dumb thing we'd done all the way.

Then we were all sent home, our fathers following us still fit to be tied, they were so mad. Brock came down with a terrible cold, but none of the rest of us were any the worse for wear, and I happen to know that Brock was coming down with his cold at breakfast and had nearly drowned himself taking nosedrops so he wouldn't sneeze and be kept in.

Of course everybody was furious with us and we were forbidden to use the dory for a month as punishment. We griped but we saw the justice of it. They were right, it *was* a stupid thing to have done, and we knew better.

We never did get to the graveyard, but we didn't mind so much after we heard that the report had been exaggerated. The sea had washed some of the concrete facing off the sea wall but hadn't breached it by a long shot, and no graves had actually been uncovered, just one corner of one coffin. So we couldn't have gotten a skull anyhow.

We spent the next three weeks collecting the goodies the storm had left, and got a huge pile of driftwood for our lobster cooking in the poison ivy patch. We also spent a good deal of time watching the carpenters repairing the beach cottages. There was a boat across the causeway and it took people a couple of weeks to get it off, so our fathers took turns driving us to school the long way around by way of Prescott Road. What with getting a ride and all the storm damage and flotsam to occupy me, I didn't see Joe again until after school stopped and we moved the dory to his yard. The boys had their traps out again on the other side of the harbor.

That year I wasn't so crazy about getting blisters and calluses rowing so I didn't go with them as often. In fact, I got out of it as much as I could and still be allowed to eat lobsters with them. One day Joe asked me why I wasn't out fishing with the boys.

"I don't know," I said, "I guess I just don't feel much like it today."

"How old are you now?" he asked.

"Twelve."

He looked at me, and said speculatively, "Jessica, I think you're growing up."

"Is that good or bad?" I asked, then had an afterthought and looked down at my chest. It was just exactly as flat as ever.

"It depends on what you make of it."

"What does that mean?"

"That you're going to have to find out who you are pretty soon. I don't envy you the job, though I think you'll not do too badly."

"I know who I am," I said rather indignantly. "I'm Jessica Brewer."

"But who is Jessica Brewer?"

"Don't tease."

"I wasn't teasing, but never mind. Let's drop it."

I was willing enough to drop it. Up until that year I'd thought that giving my address and phone number would finish the job of explaining exactly who I was. I was just beginning to realize there was a lot more to it than that but I was not yet prepared to think about it, if I didn't have to.

10

That's how it was. I'd begun to change and grow up a little, but not very much. The summer went along the way you'd expect it to, with mostly clear weather and some rain, hot spells and cool spells, and days spent on the rocks.

When weather does something important it lets you know ahead of time, if you know how to read the signs. When people do something important there's no advance warning often as not, because the people don't know they're going to do it.

One morning towards the end of July, Brock and I looked out and saw a big bank of fog rolling in off the water, thick and white as fleece. We put on slickers and boots (the fog was very cold and damp) and went to play with Bobby or one of the others, but none of them were home. We decided it wasn't worth the effort of looking for them, so after hallooing a couple of times and getting no reply, we decided to go visit Joe. (Joe was helping Brock carve a model of the dory.) Offshore we could hear the foghorns bellowing and the whistling lighthouse off Baker's Island was screeching like a steam locomotive.

We took our time walking along the road. The soft white fog muffled everything making the world strange. You could hear moisture dripping from everything as it condensed, and the sun was so faint and large a blur that we could tell the fog wouldn't burn off before noon.

It seemed as if we were the only souls abroad that day. We didn't pass anyone and the only sounds were the foghorns, the lighthouse, the lazy ringing of the bell buoy, the gulls, and from across the harbor an occasional barking of dogs. (Adonis disapproved of fog, and barked at it whenever he thought Mr. O'Brien wasn't around to correct him. This always started other dogs going.)

Then, at the crossroads where the road from the causeway joins Crescent Road, we saw the yellow blur of headlights and heard a man cursing. We were feeling a little spooky in the strangeness of the fog, so we stopped and discussed it with each other before we decided to go and see who was out there. We knew by the voice that it was a stranger, and by the accent that he was from Boston or somewhere very near there.

We went closer and all of a sudden there he was, a tall slender man in a raincoat and city hat, standing beside his car looking lost and angry. We stayed our distance, and Brock asked, "Can we help you?"

The man, who hadn't been looking in our direction, jumped when he heard Brock speak, and whirled to face us. He was very edgy but at the time we put it down to the fog and being lost and all. The stranger said he was lost and didn't know where he was. He offered the totally unnecessary information that he was not from around these parts. He said "paats" with a very flat "a" and leaving the "r" out entirely. He asked us to tell him how to get to the breakwater.

Summer people like to go to the breakwater to look at the harbor, so this didn't surprise us. It didn't even surprise us that a summer person would think he might be able to see something in the fog; it's amazing how little some city people know about things like that.

"You can't see anything from the breakwater until the fog lifts," Brock informed him helpfully.

Instead of answering to what Brock said, the man repeated his request for directions. Brock told him. He got into his car, slammed the door, and took off down the hill without a word of thanks.

We continued on our way, snailing along, wandering back and forth across the road, enjoying the feeling of being alone in the fog. The stranger's accent amused us and we spent some time thinking up words and imitating it. Brock said he'd had half a mind to send the stranger off in the wrong direction. He hadn't said which breakwater, and if Brock had pointed him in the opposite direction he would have driven fifteen miles and fetched up at the breakwater at Turner's Harbor. I wonder now what would have happened if Brock had done it.

I wonder how we looked to the stranger, two stony little faces staring out at him out of yellow slickers that covered us from head to heel, unsmiling, sober, slightly disapproving. Was he amused, irritated, a bit discouraged? Or did he see us only as convenient local inhabitants, fortuitously met in a time and place where he needed directions, no more to be considered or thought about than a signpost? He had been standing in the fog for some time; we could tell that because water was dripping off his hat and plastic raincoat, and he had left two cigarette butts on the road. I imagine him standing there smoking, wondering which way to turn, feeling that he was in a forsaken place, for there were no houses in the immediate vicinity. There were many houses along the various roads, but back then, five years ago before this recent building boom, all the houses were set well back from the road. In the fog he couldn't have seen more than trees and hedges with ambiguous beginnings of gravel driveways that could just as well have been roads leading nowhere. And of course the ubiquitous stone walls, the low kind made of round stones, that accumulate at the borders of any cultivated land in New England. The walls aren't made purposely, the way you'd set out to build a fence, they just happen. Each year rocks are heaved up by the frost and you have to put them somewhere.

In the parking area at the end of the road at the base of the breakwater we saw the stranger's cream-colored car again. It was empty, and we went out onto the breakwater to see if he was there, but there was no one, though we went the whole way to the end. We came back, and before going to Joe's house Brock had to stop and look at the car. It was a four-door late model sedan with blue leather seats and a whole lot of extra gadgets, like a thermometer and a fancy radio with a whip antenna—things like that. It had one of those plastic Madonnas with a light in her stomach stuck in the back window. It took Brock a long time to see what there was to see about the car, but finally he was through and agreed to go down to Joe's house with me. We both wondered where the stranger was, and discussed the possibility that he might have fallen off the breakwater. There isn't any path or smooth way down it (although the rough boulders it's made of are fairly level), and since they were damp they were slippery enough to be difficult to walk on. We paused to look at the water. The tide was just full and quiet as a millpond; it had not yet turned to ebb, so it didn't seem likely that the stranger had fallen in, because he could easily enough have hauled himself out again. The sides of the breakwater are far from sheer, since the boulders are just dumped, and there are rocks below water all the way around that anyone could use to climb up by. The disappearance of the stranger mystified us, but it never crossed our minds that he might be visiting Joe, because no adults ever did.

We were just coming through the fence when Joe's door sprang open and the stranger came running down the ramp out into the yard. Joe followed him in his wheelchair and chased him a few feet, then stopped. The sand in the yard was wet, which made it a better surface for the wheelchair than it did dry, and we knew that Joe could go almost as fast as we could run because he'd raced us a couple of times. The tufts of grass slowed him down though, because they stuck up higher than the rest of the yard, and I think he may have hit one which is why he stopped. He backed up a little and sat there.

Brock and I carefully and silently backed through the fence and crouched down like a pair of rabbits behind the fallen rails.

Joe said low and hoarse, "Beat it."

147

The stranger laughed. I'd thought until then that Joe's public laugh set a record for humorless, unpleasant laugher, but this one was a record-breaker by a mile. It was in a different class. Joe's laugh was harsh, cutting, sarcastic, angry, even mean, but it was as straightforward as a sock in the nose. The stranger's laugh was soft, a sort of chuckle, and it made me think of swarming maggots under a dead bird. It was seething with hate.

Brock pulled my sleeve and we quietly crept along the fence a ways, climbed through under the elderberry bushes, and crouched down under them, closer to Joe and the stranger, but better hidden by the drooping branches and the fringe of tall, coarse weeds in front of them. It was so quiet, except for the foghorns and things, that we could hear the stranger breathing and hear his raincoat rustling as he moved. They were edging around each other, Joe following in his chair and the stranger backing and circling. I wondered why Joe was moving so clumsily and slowly. Then Joe stopped, as if tired, but I could tell by his breathing that he wasn't in the least winded, it was much slower than the stranger's.

Then the stranger began to talk. A lot of it didn't make any sense to us because he was referring to events we knew nothing about. He kept mentioning "the day at the carnival" as if it meant something, but we never could figure out what it meant because neither he nor Joe said enough about the day at the carnival to make it clear. The stranger also kept saying things about how awful Joe looked, how no woman would ever be able to look at him without being nauseated, and so on. And taunting Joe about being a cripple, and not a man, and stuff like that. He kept repeating himself over and over as if saying it made him feel good.

Joe had been very angry but then he seemed to get hold of himself, he relaxed and said, "Why did you come here? Only to gloat?"

"Perhaps," the man said.

"Well, now you've gloated. Go home."

"Don't you want to hear about your son?"

"What son?"

"The son you're so busy building a bank account for. My wife's son."

"I don't know what you're talking about," Joe said in a flat, bored voice.

"Yes you do. Don't think you can put me off by denying it. I found this." He took a little brown bank-book out of his pocket and threw it to Joe.

Joe caught it and examined it, then threw it back. "I never saw it before in my life."

"Then where did the money come from?"

"How should I know?"

The stranger lost his temper. "Listen you," he screamed, "I *know* you sent the money. Bonnie told me. You hear, she admitted it."

"I don't believe you."

The stranger was almost beside himself, he held up his hands. "How do you think I got these knuckles bruised?" he yelled. "How do you think I found out where you were? I tell you, I found the bankbook, and I beat the truth out of her. She told me all right."

Joe snorted. "You always were a liar, a coward and a liar."

"I got it out of her, I tell you. She told me every-thing. How cosy you two were while I was in hospital with pneumonia; she told me everything. Everything."

"You were *not* in the hospital with pneumonia," Joe said disgustedly. "You were in the hospital malingering, trying to keep from being shipped out to Korea with the rest of the unit. And furthermore, if you'd had the guts to keep it up just one more day you'd have been transferred to the psycho ward and gotten out on a Sec-tion Eight then instead of later. And I wish you had, ten good men would be alive today if you'd stuck it out one more day."

It was about then that I realized that Joe was in a fury, that he was controlling it and goading the stranger.

The stranger called Joe a whole string of dirty names, then began saying how "that damn kid" took after Joe, and how he (the stranger) was trying to beat it out of him, but the kid was incorrigible.

"How old is the kid?" Joe asked very quietly.

"Seven, as you damn well know."

"And you expect him to mow the entire lawn?"

"It's good for him, builds character. His mother pampers him too much, he's just a no-good kid. A lousy no-good kid."

"I suppose you tell him so." Very slowly Joe was moving closer to the stranger, the stranger was appar-ently too angry to notice.

"Why shouldn't I? Sure I told him he's a little bastard, that his mother's a no-good too. Do you know what the little punk did? He called the cops on me when I was making his mother tell me about the bank-book. That's loyalty for you. Wait'll I get home! As soon as I get the cops taken care of I'll fix that little punk's wagon for him. I'll teach him to be loyal to the man who's fed and clothed him. I'll fix Bonnie too."

It went on like that for a while, Joe edging closer and closer, saying just enough to keep the stranger mad enough not to really notice. Then, suddenly as a snake striking, Joe grabbed the stranger with both hands and before I quite knew how he'd done it, lifted him high in the air and brought him down, backfirst across one arm of the wheelchair. There was a sound rather like a rotten branch breaking, only different, and the man screamed horribly. Up until then I'd been hating the stranger and rooting for Joe, hoping he'd catch him and teach him a lesson, but after he screamed it was as if everything had turned upside down; it was only then that I realized what I'd been wishing, and I felt as if all my insides had shriveled up like a prune. I wanted to call out, "No, I didn't mean for you to break him, please stop and let him go," but I could no more have made a sound than I could have turned into a bird and flown away.

Holding the stranger across his lap Joe said very quietly, "Shut up," and to my amazement the man did. His eyes were white all the way around the iris and his face was gray. His hat had fallen off.

"Don't kill me," he said, begging. "Please don't kill me. I'll give Bonnie a divorce, you can have her, and the kid too. Everything, you can have anything you want, just don't kill me."

"You are a liar," Joe said very coldly and dispassionately, like a bookkeeper stating the total of an account in a ledger. "If I don't kill you, you'll go home and make life hell for Bonnie and the boy."

The stranger began to plead even harder, waving his

arms feebly, and tears were dripping down his cheeks, promising Joe all kinds of things.

"Why did you beat the boy?" Joe asked finally.

"For his own good, it was only for his own good."

"You always were self-righteous," Joe said in that dispassionate bookkeeper's voice. Then he added, "I've broken your back, you know. You may die anyway."

At this the man began to actually wring his hands. He was sobbing and begging and feebly struggling as if to get away, but his back was broken at the waist, and he couldn't move his legs or body.

I was shivering and my teeth ached from clenching them to keep them from chattering. I leaned close to Brock for warmth and we put our arms around each other the way we used to when we were real little. Brock was shivering too. I whispered in his ear, "What should we do?"

"I don't know," he whispered back.

Joe told the man, very coldly, that the more he struggled the worse the damage to his back would be, and the stranger suddenly became very still. Joe turned the wheelchair around and began wheeling it towards the beach. It is a hard, narrow gravel beach and the chair hardly sank in at all. The tide was just beginning to ebb and the waves were lapping softly high up, so Joe hadn't far to go. He drove the chair into the water and set the brake hard. The man saw the water and began pleading again, saying over and over, "I'll be good, please don't kill me." I couldn't help feeling sorry for him and I hoped Joe wouldn't do it.

Joe said, "I should have done it years ago," and lifted the stranger over his head and threw him into the water. When Joe lifted him the stranger made a strange choking, gasping sound, as if he was trying to scream but couldn't get the breath to do it. Then there was a splash and that was all, the stranger must have sunk like a stone, sucked down by the ebb current.

Joe sat there a long time, so long that the waves had retreated past him and he was on dry beach before he moved. Then he came back towards the house and looked at the yard. There were sharp, clear prints all over it, the impressions standing out clearly in the damp sand. Joe picked up the stranger's hat and sailed it far out into the fog over the water, then he got out the hose and washed down the yard and all the way from the edge of the road to the beach and back and forth by the front door. When he was done, there was nothing to be seen but the marks of his own tires. He turned the hose off and went back into the house.

It was as if Brock and I were paralysed until Joe was out of sight. We sat there hugging each other under the dripping bushes, clenching our teeth to keep them from chattering. Then, the moment we heard Joe's door latch, we were suddenly galvanized into action. We scurried back to the parking area and ran down the breakwater, looking to see if perhaps the stranger had not been killed but had managed to hold on to a rock. There was nothing but the lapping of water, the fog-horns, the bell buoy, the barking of Adonis and the whistling of the Baker's Island lighthouse. High above the gulls were complaining about the fog, and down the beach the sandpipers were prospecting as if nothing had happened.

"He's dead for sure," Brock said finally.

"I guess he must be," I agreed.

We stood looking down into the cold green water,

imagining the body being swept around the end of the breakwater and out to sea. We were still shivering.

"I'm freezing to death," Brock said.

"So am I."

We both together started for home at a dead run. We passed the cream-colored car and kept on running until we had to stop for breath. Then we walked the rest of the way home, panting, not talking. Neither one of us could have said how we felt, I think. I know that I couldn't believe it. It was too extraordinary and awful.

I couldn't eat any lunch, and because of the way I was still shivering Mom put me to bed with a heating pad. Brock ate lunch but urped it afterwards, so Mom put him to bed too with the other heating pad. I felt as if I'd never be warm again as long as I lived, and Brock said he felt the same way. We both had the urps all afternoon and couldn't eat any supper. Dad decided we had flu and called Doc Elsinger, who prescribed aspirin and bedrest and stayed for a cup of coffee.

He and Dad were sitting on the couch that's against the stair wall, and the well is right above it, so even if you don't try, you can hear everthing anyone sitting there says. For some reason Doc got to talking about Joe, and of course, the minute I heard his name I just had to come creeping out of bed and into the hall to listen. I found Brock already there. He had his blanket with him and I'd forgotten mine, so I got inside it with him, and we crouched there listening.

"He's a co-operative enough patient," Doc was saying, "but I always have the feeling that he has no faith in me at all. . . . At first I thought it was because I'm a G.P. in a small town; after all the man's been accustomed to every expert in the book. . . . But now I don't think so."

There was a pause and Dad asked, "Do you have any idea what it is?" (Dad and Doc were buddies from way back.)

"A couple of months ago he made a remark about doctors that think they know everything but can't explain it when something goes wrong. This was, incidentally, by way of an oblique compliment. . . . I'd just finished telling him I didn't know something or other . . . can't recall what off-hand, something minor . . . the effects of a new drug I think. I have a notion that he has no faith in doctors, or to be more accurate, he is far too aware of the limitations of medicine. Have you ever spoken to him, Tom?"

"Only to say hello on the street."

"He has a metal prosthesis in his mouth that would fascinate you; I've never seen anything like it," Doc said parenthetically, then asked, to the point, "What do you think of him?"

"I don't know him well enough to have an opinion about him. He seems to have alienated most of the village."

At this point Mom said, "He gets on very well with the kids. They've been keeping their dory in his yard."

"If only he wouldn't laugh . . ." Doc said rather plaintively.

"Has he laughed at you?" Dad asked.

"Once, but I deserved it. I'd made a rather pompous remark to the effect that I was there to help him. . . . It deserved a horselaugh. . . ." (Doc has a habit of sort of letting his sentences trail off sometimes.) There was a pause, then Doc said thoughtfully, "It's discouraging that there's so little that can be done for St. George.

He's in almost constant pain, but I can't give him opiates and nothing else seems to help much. . . . I tell myself that he may live quite a few years yet and I'd be doing him no favor to make an addict of him. . . . The first time I visited him he told me he'd been through withdrawal once and had no intention whatsoever of going through it again. Said he'd sue me if he ever caught me giving him narcotics."

"That sounds masochistic," Dad said.

"Not at all in this case . . . just very realistic. He said he'd save opiates for later, when they were really needed, and he's probably right. . . . From his point of view at least."

"His point of view?" Mom asked.

"He expects to live five or ten more years at least. . . . He could be right, it's possible. . . ."

"How long do you give him?" Dad asked.

"That would be hard to say. . . . Two or three years at the outside. . . . It wouldn't surprise me if he died tomorrow. But you never can tell, and even if I were certain. . . . How could I tell him that he hasn't enough time left for it to matter what drugs he takes?"

"I guess you couldn't," Dad agreed.

Then they started talking about something else and Brock and I went into the bathroom to discuss what we'd heard. Neither of us had known most of what Doc had said about Joe.

Then Brock said, "What do you think we ought to do?"

"Do?" It hadn't occurred to me that we ought to do anything.

"You're supposed to report it when somebody murders somebody."

That was the first time either of us had said the word "murder" and it sort of echoed in our ears, shocking both of us, because saying the word made it suddenly real, instead of a sort of bad dream. The whole thing had been so dream-like in the silence and fog, with the two figures englobed in a white, featureless kind of nothingness, the sandy yard, and an edge of the sea, and vaguely in the background the side of the house, all you could see except for them.

Impulsively, without thinking, I said, "Don't tell, Brock."

"If we don't that makes us accessories."

"What's accessories?"

"Somebody who knows about a crime and doesn't tell, stupid."

"If you're so smart tell me how we're supposed to explain why we sat there like a pair of bumps on a log and didn't do a single, solitary thing to stop it."

This threw Brock into a brown study. Finally he said tentatively, "We could say we were afraid?"

"Were we?"

"Shut up, you sound like Mom."

I didn't say anything; I waited Brock out, and after a while he said sarcastically, "*I* was afraid, I don't know about you."

"Sure I was, what do you *think*? But is that why we didn't even say anything?"

After a while Brock admitted, "I don't know. I think I *wanted* Joe to do something to the stranger—up to the point where he did, and then after that it was too late."

"You could have called out before Joe heaved him into the water."

"Why didn't *you*?"

"I don't know. It didn't occur to me. That's all, it just didn't occur to me."

Brock doesn't sidetrack easily. "We ought to report it," he said.

"What good would that do?"

"You're *supposed* to."

"Supposed, supposed, what *good* would it do? Besides, who'd believe us?"

"They'll believe us when the body washes up at Turner's Harbor."

"Then there's no point telling before it washes up."

"Maybe not."

"So let's wait anyhow until then. All right?"

"Why are you so dead set against telling?"

"Well gee-whiz, who would it make happier? The stranger's wife and kid? From what he said, they're better off without him, they'll probably be glad he's gone. Would they like to know Joe killed him? What about the little kid? Would you like everybody to know your Dad was a murderer?" Brock shook his head. "And if we tell any of it we'll have to tell all of it, and how would *that* make Bonnie and the kid feel? Even if we didn't, I bet they'd find out once they started looking for a motive. And how would Joe feel? And besides, you heard what Doc Elsinger said, Joe's dying anyway. What good would having him arrested do? Do you want him to suffer more than he is already? How mean can you get?"

"All right, all right," Brock broke in. "I promise I won't tell for now anyway. Will you shut up about it?"

We hassled it around a lot more, both then and later.

11

Two days after that we heard that the abandoned car had been noticed and Chief King had been out to check up on it. Bobby had been on his way to the poison ivy with a sack of shorts and had been scared half to death when he saw the Chief coming up the path toward him. He thought he was finally getting caught for keeping short lobsters. He took off and threw the lobsters back into the ocean, then he calmed down enough to realize that nobody had chased him and got curious. When he went back all he discovered, though, was that Chief King was going to impound the car.

Brock and I discussed it, and after lunch we got some good driftwood to provide an excuse and went into the village on our bikes. We knew that if we went into the Lobster Pot without an excuse Mrs. Root would shoo us out, but that if we had something to sell she'd make us wait until she got through talking. It drove us crazy when we were really interested in selling her something, but this time it was exactly what we wanted. We parked our bikes beside the Lobster Pot and waited to go in until we saw one of the deputies go in.

The deputy said that Chief King had consulted the "hot sheet" and the car wasn't stolen, but its owner was wanted by the police of a small town near Boston. The charge against the stranger was "assault with intent to kill" and his wife and kid were in the hospital with broken arms and bruises. I remember wondering why the stranger was so crazy about breaking arms, he'd broken both of his wife's. The deputy said he'd done it the evening of the day before the fog.

Chief King had checked the ground around the car, but of course there was nothing to find. He'd even spoken to Joe, but Joe said he hadn't seen anyone. Mr. Mullins, who runs the gas station, said that a tall man with a cream sedan and a Boston accent had asked the way to the breakwater shortly before the fog had begun to roll in. The Chief had Mr. Mullins look at the car, and Mr. Mullins said it was the same one; he recognized a scratch on one fender because he remembered wondering what had left orange paint in the scratch. And of course there was also the whip antenna and the Madonna of the Road in the back window. It was an easy car to remember.

The guess was that the stranger had come to the breakwater during the fog, had gone out on it, and had slipped and fallen into the water. There was some speculation as to why the stranger had wanted to go to the breakwater, but not very much; it was the kind of illogical thing city people seemed to do. The Chief had said that the tide had turned to ebb about half an hour after the fog came in, and the stranger would have had to fall in sometime after that because otherwise he either wouldn't have drowned or else would have already showed up in the salt-marsh. The deputy said the Chief had said he bet the stranger was wearing slick-soled leather shoes. I whispered to Brock, "Was he? I don't remember."

Brock nodded, "I'm almost sure he was."

Looking out the window of the Lobster Pot we could see men searching around the breakwater, which was, at that time of day, partly uncovered by the low tide. (They didn't find anything, but nobody had expected them to.)

In spite of my wanting to protect Joe I had the most awful urge to speak up and tell the adults that I knew all about what had happened to the stranger, that I could answer all their questions. I imagined them not believing me and then coming to apologize when the body showed up at Turner's Harbor with a broken back.

Mrs. Root finally bought our driftwood and we had to leave the Lobster Pot, but we'd learned what we'd come to find out. On the way to the causeway we passed the Irish priest in his neat suit walking down the sidewalk beside the French priest in his cassock, which was billowing out in the breeze like a spinnaker. They were talking about the stranger, the first time I ever saw them speak to each other. They say "It's an ill wind that blows no good."

When we were out onto the causeway where no one could overhear us I said, "He was a real monster. I'm *glad* Joe killed him."

"I'm not," Brock said sombrely. "I could wish he'd

fallen off the breakwater of his own accord and been drowned, but I wish Joe hadn't done it. Oh how I wish Joe hadn't done it!"

"Everybody's already decided exactly how it happened, how the stranger walked out in his city shoes, slipped, and fell in during the ebb. When he washes up on the clamflats there won't be anything to indicate that wasn't what happened. Why don't we just pretend everybody's right and forget the whole thing?"

"I wish I *could* forget the whole thing," Brock said feelingly. "By stomach still gets cold shivers when I think about it."

"Me too."

"Jessica, it's our duty as citizens to tell."

"Would that make your stomach feel any better?"

"It might."

"Foof!" I knew that was nonsense, and I was annoyed with Brock for being so dense. It seemed to me he was doing it on purpose.

"Can't you see?" Brock said intensely. "If we don't tell we're to blame too. We've got the stranger's blood on our hands too, because we watched and didn't do anything—and then didn't tell."

"Telling isn't going to wash away a heck of a lot of blood," I snapped. "Besides, the stranger wasn't bleeding." It was the memory of his tears that troubled me, but I wasn't going to mention that to Brock, he had too much ammunition already.

"Don't be stupid," Brock snapped.

We came to the end of the causeway and stopped talking while we pedaled uphill. At the crossroads, the same place we'd met the stranger in the fog, we paused to get our breath. I looked around, and the crossroads seemed like a totally different place from the one where we had met a man with a Boston accent lost in the fog. Everything was dry, a brisk wind blew singing through the long grass and the leaves of the elms sparkled in the sunlight. A garter snake was slowly sliding along the stone wall by the road, shiny and elegant in a new skin. The air was full of the drowsy scent of field flowers, their odor extracted by the warm sun.

"We can pretend it didn't happen," I said. In spite of my continued opposition to Brock, though, I was beginning to weaken. I'd spent most of my life following where he led and it had been very rare that I had ever opposed him, and I never had on something important. It was always easier to go along with him.

Brock knows me pretty well and he knew I was beginning to give in. Instead of crowing, which would have been fatal to getting his own way, he reaffirmed his earlier promise, "Anyway, we won't say anything until the body shows up."

I sighed. I really didn't want to tell, but I could see I was probably going to at least agree that Brock was telling the truth when he told. I imagined all the adult attention. It had seemed appealing back at the Lobster Pot, but now it seemed endlessly boring and bothersome. I imagined being asked why we hadn't said anything, or called out, and knew we had no good answer. If we said we were too afraid that might make things even worse for Joe because, knowing how people think, they'd go around saying Joe frightened children. We had been afraid, but it hadn't been that kind of fear. If we'd called out, Joe couldn't have caught us, even assuming he might have wanted to, because he couldn't possibly have driven his chair through the bushes and

163

by the time he went around to where he could go through the gap in the fence, we could have been half-way home. I think now that rather than what one usually thinks of as fear, we'd felt the kind of paralysis of horror people feel in the face of catastrophe. For a child it is a catastrophe for an adult they like and respect to do something dreadful.

Brock had gotten tired of waiting for me and was inching his bike along toward home. "Come along," he said and put his feet on the pedals and started off.

"In a minute," I called, and watched him out of sight around the curve. Then I turned towards Joe's house and coasted down the hill.

The top half of the Dutch door was open and Joe called to me to come in. He was in bed, very white around the mouth. He said that Doc Elsinger had been there, when I said something indicating I was worried about him, and that it was just that his back was acting up a little bit. I remember wondering if he'd hurt himself when he'd picked the stranger up like that, or when he'd thrown him in the water.

There was a bunch of unopened new magazines on the foot of his bed, and a little package of microfilm from the Library of Congress. I asked if I could sit on the bed. Joe said, "Go ahead, only don't joggle it," so I sat in the wheelchair instead. It was very comfortable. It felt odd to sit in it; I never had before. This was the first time I'd seen Joe out of it, as a matter of fact, and I remember being surprised at how very long he was stretched out flat.

I asked if he minded my sitting in his chair, and he said not at all, and seemed to mean it. Once, the winter before, Joe had asked us if Brock and I would like

164

chairs to sit on, but we'd said no. We preferred sitting on tables; we weren't allowed to at home or any place else for that matter. I was also afraid that if we'd let him build or buy chairs, that he'd maybe have other people there to sit in them, and I wanted him to myself. I realize now that was selfish of me, but back then it wouldn't have occurred to me.

Joe was different that day. He seemed worn out, and he acted more glad to see me than ever before. He held my hand, I remember, for a few minutes, then said, "You're a good kid Jessica. A real good kid. Don't—" there was a long pause and he finished "—think too badly of me."

"I won't," I said with a promptness that surprised him. I think now that that was the exact moment when I made up my mind for sure that I was not going to tell, and that I'd move heaven and earth to keep Brock from telling.

Joe looked at me oddly, seemed about to ask a question, then decided he'd better not. I wonder if he ever guessed that I knew what he'd done? I think he didn't, but if he ever came close to guessing, that was the time. I think he might have guessed if he hadn't wanted so badly to believe that no one knew.

At the time my decision seemed sudden, sort of out of the clear blue. One minute I was hesitating, and the next I wasn't. At the time I couldn't possibly have said what it was that made up my mind. Now as I look back I think it was, partly anyway, that I could see Joe was in pain. He didn't say anything, but he kept moving his head and shoulders restlessly, as if he couldn't manage to get comfortable, and his face was drawn. I think that was the first time I ever felt really sorry for him.

I don't mean hurting for him, which is semi-automatic with me and extends to even mice. I think what I mean is feeling compassion. The way I felt when Brock had to kill the hurt mouse; I hurt for the mouse, but I was sorry for Brock, that's the best I can do to explain. And it wasn't just that, sitting in his wheelchair, I got an inkling of what it might feel like to be him and not able to walk, run, or ride a bike. It was far more than that.

It wasn't even simply that I realized that even a dragon-slayer sometimes needs protection, although I suppose that entered into it. At the time I simply decided, sort of the way I'd decided Joe was *the* St. George, that I wasn't going to let Brock tell or persuade me to tell, and at the time I didn't know why I decided that way. Now, looking back, I think I know. I think the major reason was that if Joe knew I knew he'd killed the stranger, it would have become impossible for me to be friends with him. To have told would have been to lose Joe, even if nobody had believed us, even if he hadn't been prosecuted or taken away to jail. And being Joe's friend wasn't just a kid thing any more either, because it was then that I realized how much he needed me. Brock and the others too. And even though it was frightening sometimes, it was a good feeling too because I knew I was important to somebody. Life-and-death important.

The Turner Harbor police and the Coast Guard had been alerted to expect a body on the clamflats. There was a brief half-hearted attempt to drag the harbor. Nobody expected to find it there. It was one of those things people do for form's sake. In spite of the alert, the body washed in sometime during the night

166

and was only found by the Coast Guard in the middle of the next day. By that time the crabs and gulls had been at it and it was almost unrecognizable. I guess the fish had done their bit too during the week it had been in the water.

There was a good deal of consternation because the body was almost torn in half. But the coroner from the county seat came down and autopsied and said "Death by drowning," and that closed the case. There was salt water and seaweed in the lungs. Everybody said that the stranger must have broken his back when he slipped on the breakwater, and then drowned. By then it was known that he was a strong swimmer. One faction disagreed and said it had happened when the body was dragged along the bottom by the ebb current. They asked the coroner, but he said that by this time there was no way to tell one way or the other. This started a village-wide argument that still crops up from time to time. The Irish priest and French priest disagreed and stopped speaking to each other again.

A lot of people take a kind of pride in the ebb current. They act almost as if they'd invented it, and talk almost gleefully, and certainly respectfully, of its strength and savagery—as if its existence somehow reflected credit on them. They seemed pleased (even while deploring it) with this, its most recent accomplishment.

But the point is that nobody ever suspected for a minute that the death wasn't accidental. The deputy pointed out, proudly, that Chief King had been correct, the stranger was wearing slick leather-soled city shoes (one had stayed on) and everybody went around congratulating the Chief on his acumen.

What the stranger was doing on the breakwater in

the first place remained an unsolved mystery as far as the village was concerned. Chief King even made a trip to the stranger's home town to interview his widow, but she said she had no idea where he had gone, that he had run away when he heard the boy on the phone calling the police, and hadn't said where he was going. (But if she knew where Joe lived, she must have known where the stranger was going, and what he was doing there. She must have guessed what really happened.)

Brock still wanted to tell. As soon as the coroner gave the official verdict of "Death by misadventure" Brock was all set to go barreling off to Chief King to tell him all about it. He wanted me to go with him to back him up.

I said, "All right, I'll go. But if you tell, do you know what I'll do? I'll say that you made it all up, that the morning of the fog we were out on the rocks nowhere near the breakwater and that you just want to make yourself important."

Brock was appalled. "You wouldn't!"

"Yes I would, and you know as well as I do who they'll believe."

"Why should they believe you instead of me? I'm older."

"But I'd be saying what they *want* to hear, and you wouldn't. Do you think Chief King wants to hear that his guess about the shoes is completely beside the point? Do you think that all the people who've been saying how they knew it all along will want to look stupid?"

Brock looked at me as if I'd turned green with pink polkadots. "You *can't* lie like that!"

To give him the idea, I looked as innocent as possible (which is pretty darn innocent, believe me) and asked in a bewildered tone, "Lie like what? I don't understand."

"You know we saw it!"

"Saw what? I didn't see anything. We were down by the house-rock catching white snails all morning."

"There, I got you," Brock crowed. "The tide was still way in."

"Thank you," I said.

Brock's face fell, he looked as if he wanted to kick himself. He realized that if he'd kept his big mouth shut I just might have gotten trapped in a lie, but now he knew I certainly wouldn't forget the state of the tide again.

"We were collecting driftwood," I said. "Down around the end of the point."

At this Brock lost his temper and punched me in the nose and made it bleed, so I punched him back and made his nose bleed too. We had one of the worst fights we've ever had, pounding each other and crying. But when it was over and Brock had won, he said, "All right, we won't tell." I guess winning the fight made him feel better.

As soon as we'd got cleaned up we wrote our document and hid it, finally, under the corner of the tool shed. I don't think Brock ever understood why I was so dead set against telling, and back then I couldn't explain because I didn't know why myself. I expect I'll show this to Brock when I've finished it. I hope that then he'll understand. I think that's been one of the reasons for that distance between us that I mentioned. It was the first time we'd ever had differing opinions of such strength, and maybe it was that both of us had to realize that we weren't sort of extensions of each other, but separate individuals.

I suppose we'd have had to realize that sooner or later anyway, but I wish it hadn't happened so soon because is was lonely. I was too young to have to stand all alone on my own two feet; at least I felt as if I was. And I couldn't even turn to Mom or Dad because of keeping the secret about what Joe had done. And of course, above all, I couldn't turn to Joe.

A day or so after the stranger washed up on the clam-flats, the *Mackerel Cove Defender* came out with a story about it. There was a picture of the stranger, a big grinning campaign picture showing him smiling a big white grin and looking Foursquare and Reliable and Everybody's Choice for Selectman. If anything it made me glad Joe'd killed him, because it was a hair-raising thought to think of him in a position of any power (though I suppose after the beating he'd given his wife and kid he wouldn't have been elected anyway. But you never know, he might have managed somehow, if not then, later, and if not in that town, perhaps in an-other one.) The paper said he'd been in the Army and in Korea. There was no mention of a Section Eight or of his having been responsible for the death of ten men, but I think the paper's information came from campaign literature so it figures. It did say he'd "seen action" in Korea and been given a medical discharge. The date showed that he'd gotten it very shortly after Joe's unit hit Korea.

I wonder if Joe knew about the baby before or after Korea. I wonder when he began sending money for the kid's bank account.

Anyway, right after the verdict of dead by misadventure was made official, Joe went back to the V.A. hospital in an ambulance. Doc Elsinger said that some of the metal in him was acting up. Joe was gone all winter and came back the next spring.

While he was gone I thought a lot about him and wondered if I'd be able to go visit him and talk comfortably the way I had before. Knowledge of the murder lay in my mind like a stone, and I kept tripping over it mentally, no matter how hard I tried to avoid it. But after a while I got used to it, and since I was very interested in forgetting it anyway, it wasn't too long before I more or less managed to. By the time Joe returned I was an expert on avoiding it, and most of the time I was able to simply pretend he hadn't done it, that I'd simply had a bad dream. It wasn't always easy; there were times when I was with Joe when I'd find myself crying out inside my mind, "Why did the stranger have to cry? If only he hadn't been crying!" because that was the thing that made it so terrible. And I'd have to remind myself that Bonnie, who obviously must have known approximately what happened, had protected Joe, and I'd have to remember all the reasons for not telling.

Joe noticed the change in me; he even commented once or twice on my absent-mindedness. And I think he noticed the change in our friendship, though he never commented on that. It was no longer as simple and straightforward as before, and there was a kind of distance between us that hadn't been there before. But he probably set that down to my getting older.

In many ways Joe was much the same. He still avoided town, talked about ships, and he still was making his pirates and slavers and corking them up one by one in bottles. The main difference in him was that from that time on he seemed tired, he didn't have the energy he'd had before, and as time went on he seemed more and more tired. Nor were his hands quite as steady, so it now took him twice as long to complete a ship.

Two years ago, around Christmas time, he had to go back to the hospital again, rather suddenly, so I didn't have a chance to say goodbye, but heard from Doc Elsinger that he'd had to go because the keloid tissue on his back was becoming cancerous. I hadn't been seeing as much of Joe after I'd started high-school, and I remember feeling guilty for neglecting him to such an extent that I didn't even know he was ill until I heard that an ambulance had come for him.

Joe returned in the middle of the following summer, tireder and more drawn than before, and somehow he seemed smaller, less burly, as if he had less muscle (though he still could chin himself with one hand, and seemed to have the same extraordinary strength in his arms).

Several days after he returned he handed me a miniature figurehead of the *Flying Cloud,* a winged angel with a golden trumpet. It was more beautifully carved than anything he'd ever made, painted and gilded very carefully. He seemed embarrassed and admitted that he'd thought he wasn't going to make it this time. They'd had to do more surgery. I wrapped the figurehead in a handkerchief and put it in a box. I still have it.

Then last summer, the last summer he was here, I almost told him I knew what he'd done and forgave him. But then I reconsidered and didn't say anything. I decided that my forgiveness didn't mean all that much, and he'd feel awful if he knew I'd seen what happened and been frightened. At least that was what I told myself my reasons were at the time. Now I know it was because I knew our friendship couldn't survive his knowing I knew.

As the summer wore on Joe became thinner and thinner. I could almost see him wasting away in front of me, but towards the middle of August he seemed to have more energy again and seemed far less tired. This pleased me, and I began to hope that he wasn't dying after all. He seemed much better, more relaxed, and he no longer acted as if it hurt him to move more than just his hands. His hands were completely steady again too, and he rapidly completed a brig that he'd been working on off and on for three months.

Then Doc Elsinger came to dinner and I heard him talking to Dad and Mom. I was sitting in a comfortable chair reading and they were having coffee on the front porch. My chair was just inside the screened front door, and I could hear everything without trying.

I don't remember how the subject of Joe came up; I wasn't listening to them, I was busy reading, but the thing that caught my attention was Dad saying that Joe lived like a hermit.

"Yes," Doc agreed, "and that's a desolate spot out there by the breakwater with no houses in sight."

"You can see the entire village across the harbor," Mom reminded him.

"I meant no neighbors," Doc amended. "In winter it depressed me just to go out there. . . . The sea is so

173

loud. . . . It seems sometimes to be about to batter down the house. St. George says he likes it though, and everyone to his own taste. . . ."

"How's he doing?" Dad asked.

"He's dying," Doc said flatly, "and he knows it. He's on opiates now. . . . Has been for several weeks."

My heart contracted and got very small and cold inside me. I had the impulse to run out onto the porch and shake Doc and yell in his face and make him take it back, make him tell me it wasn't true, that the sharp improvement in Joe was not due to drugs, but to his really being better. I closed the book on my finger and sat very still, listening.

"The trouble is," Doc was saying, "I've come to like the man. . . . He has a great deal of courage. . . . He even has the courage to face his own death without whining and without making a big thing out of it. . . . He's very bitter, but no more so now than he was before he knew his time was so very limited."

"Have you any idea why he chooses to live as he does, with no contact with people?" Dad asked.

"I wouldn't say no contact. . . . He sees a great deal of the children. . . . Your daughter in particular. He has spoken of her once or twice with a great deal of affection. . . ."

"Yes, we know she goes there," Mom said. "I guess we hadn't realized just how much time she did spend there though. She doesn't talk about him very much."

"Why should she? He rarely talks about himself. . . . Seems absorbed in his preoccupation with sailing ships. . . . He has encyclopedic knowledge about them."

"I wonder why he only wants to know the children?" Mom said.

174

"He said something once that led me to believe that he feels the children don't expect anything of him. . . . That the children do not, as adults do, pity him. They accept him on his own terms and are willing to let him simply be himself. . . . Adults don't readily accept people as they are without asking questions."

"That's true enough," Dad agreed.

"From things he's said. . . . I surmise that St. George believes himself to be contaminated by death. . . . Once when I asked him what he used to do for a living, he said, 'I'm a professional killer. That's all I know, all I've ever done; kill, learn how to kill more efficiently, and teach other men how to kill. I'm an expert on the subject, and I do it very well.' He seemed more bitter than proud. . . . And later in the same conversation he talked about K-9 Corps dogs that couldn't be retrained after the war and had to be destroyed." There was a pause; from the sounds, Doc was drinking his coffee and lighting his pipe. Then he said, "As for his relationship with the children. . . . He seems to have the notion that children are immune to what he considers his contamination. . . . The pure in heart are supposed to be immune to evil, I believe. . . ."

"In most cultures," Dad said, "certainly in ours."

Doc then went on to say, medically speaking, Joe ought to be back in the hospital, but that he wanted to stay on at Mackerel Cove as long as possible, and that Doc agreed he could. "After all . . . he might as well enjoy the little time he has left. . . . Going back wouldn't prolong his life more than a week or so at best anyway. He loves that house. . . . And, don't take this wrong, Tom, he loves Jessica. . . . Those kids mean a lot to him."

175

I didn't hear any more; I had to go up to my room and close the door so nobody would hear me crying.

The last time I saw Joe was the last week of August, the day before he went back to the hospital for the last time. It was a dry, golden day, and I'd brought Joe an armful of goldenrod. It wasn't in full bloom yet, the flowers towards the ends of the little stemlets were tiny golden brushes, but down near the main stem they were still yellow-green buds. Joe was in bed, as he had been on and off for the past week and a half, and I could almost smell death in the room, it was so obvious all over him.

The sea was very quiet that day, breaking softly and gently. I could hear the regular thud of far-off artillery fire, the Navy doing target practice over the horizon. The room was warm and full of sunlight.

I offered to put the goldenrod in water, but Joe told me not to, so I put it down on the bedside table and then sat down in the wheelchair, as I always did when Joe was in bed.

"I'm leaving tomorrow," he said after a short pause while I settled myself.

I'd been expecting it, but it was a shock anyway. "I wish you didn't have to," I said.

"It doesn't matter." He picked up a stalk of goldenrod and looked at it, then dropped it on the table again. "Do you still want me to make you the *Flying Cloud*?"

"You haven't finished the slavers and pirates."

"No, but they don't matter any more. It was a silly idea in the first place. I don't know why I thought of it."

"Don't make the *Flying Cloud*," I said impulsively. I still wanted it dreadfully, but suddenly I realized that every moment he worked on it he would be thinking of his own death, and I couldn't bear it. "I'm bigger now," I explained, "I don't need a ship any more."

"You are a big girl now," he said, looking at me. "You've almost grown up."

"I guess so." I didn't feel very grown up just then, and I was very sad because I knew I'd never see him again. I had made up my mind not to cry though, and not to act sad if I could help it. It was clear to me that Joe wanted me to pretend along with him that he wasn't dying, and I didn't want to let him down. "Do you want me to write you at the hospital?" I asked.

"No, please don't. Letters aren't the same thing. I never write letters." He paused, then said, "Jessica? What would you do if you had this house?"

"Huh?" The question took me by surprise. "I don't know," I said. "Gee-whiz, what would *I* do with a house?"

"You might want a house when you grow up."

"Yes, but gee—it would be awful to have one *now*. I mean, who wants to know they're going to have to live in a certain place when they grow up? Maybe I'll want to go live somewhere else, like New York or something."

"I expect you're right," he said. "It would be like a chain on your leg, wouldn't it? Well, it was just a passing thought."

There was a silence, the far-off gunfire had stopped. Joe didn't seem to have anything more to say. He seemed very far away that afternoon, as if he had already passed some invisible boundary on the other side of life. To fill up the time and help the afternoon to be ordinary, I began telling Joe how Brock and Oakley and Bobby were all trying to get into the same college, but Bobby's grades weren't very good. Oakley and Brock were hoping that between them they could tutor Bobby enough over the summer so he'd do better in the senior year at high-school, so he could get in next fall. "That's why they haven't been around much this summer, they've been getting all white and pale sitting in the house trying to cram Bobby full of logarithms and solid geometry. Bobby just doesn't have the knack for it, though."

Joe smiled. "If anyone can your brother can. I've never seen such a persistent kid—except you."

"I'm a fly-by-night compared to Brock."

"Are you going to college?"

"Mom and Dad are planning on it. And I want to. You know, it's funny. Just last summer Mackerel Cove seemed as big a place as anyone could want, but this summer it's gotten smaller. I'd like to go somewhere else and see different people and not know everybody's name, address, and ancestry."

"You don't know the summer people."

"They don't count."

"They're the people who live in the rest of the world; maybe you'd better start counting them."

"A bunch of landlubbers."

"Knowing the sea isn't everything, Jessica. The landlubbers know things worth knowing too."

"I hadn't thought of that," I said, then, thinking, added, "Jeepers, maybe I'll seem as dumb to them in their towns as they seem to me in mine—I sure hope they have more patience than I do."

"Patience is not one of your virtues," Joe said, but kindly enough and with a smile so I didn't mind. Then he said, "Don't worry, you'll always be all right, I can tell."

178

Then before I could ask him how he could tell, he told me to bring him a coke and asked me if I'd like one too. That was one of things I liked about Joe. Most adults, when they say, "Would you like to do thus and so?" don't mean, "Would you like to" at all. They mean "go and do what I say, like it or not." They don't give a whoop if you'd "like" to, they just put it that way so they won't have to notice that they're ordering you around. If you point out that you would *not* "like" to, but will do it anyway, then they get mad. Joe, if he asked me if I'd like to get a coke, meant exactly what he said. When he meant "go and get one" he *said* to go and get one, with no nonsensing around about "liking" to get one.

We drank the coke, and I couldn't help remembering that he'd given me coke the first time I'd met him. We talked. About everything except the one thing we were both thinking about, the fact of his leaving. I told him I thought I wanted to be a doctor when I grew up, and he said that was a worthy ambition. He described the Golden Gate Bridge and talked some about San Francisco. We talked a bit about ships and about crabs—"shoes and ships and sealingwax, and cabbages and kings. . . ." Then it began to get late.

"Isn't it time for you to be getting home?" Joe asked.

"Yes, I'd better be going, I'm already late for supper," I agreed, but didn't make a move to go. The sun had left the polished, carpetless floor and was beginning to climb the wall.

"Say goodbye to Brock for me," Joe said. "And give my best to Oakley and Bobby and the others. Tell them I wish them good luck."

"O.K. I will."

There was a long silence. Joe knew I knew he was dying, that we'd never see each other again. After a time, he said, "Forget me, Jessica. Go home and forget you ever knew me."

"Why?"

"Why not?"

"I won't forget you, not ever," I said soberly, struggling with the lump in my throat. "I couldn't forget you even if I tried, even if I wanted to."

"All right," he said. It was very quiet and the house echoed faintly to the sound of the surf on the breakwater. Outside the gulls were crying in the dusk.

Suddenly I felt tears pricking behind my eyeballs, and the lump in my throat was so big it hurt. I knew I'd better get out of there before I cried and spoiled everything. "Well . . ." I said inconclusively, "goodbye then. Have a good trip."

Joe put out his hand and I took hold of it. It was warm and dry, pleasant to the touch. It surprised me, because somehow I'd expected it to be cold. "Wish me, rather, a short and easy trip," he said in his teasing voice. "The trip I'm taking is never a good one." I couldn't reply, my voice had completely deserted me. Joe gave my hand a squeeze and let go of it. "Goodbye," he said. "Be sure to shut the door after you."

I nodded and left. Outside I began to cry, and cried all the way home. I guess that explains why I didn't feel much of anything when I got the news Joe St. George was dead. I'd already done most of my mourning for him. I'd already said goodbye.

12

So that is the story of Joe St. George, and I've tried very hard to remember everything, and not to fudge just because I'd rather not think about some things. It's August again now, and nearly time for school to start again. Brock's all involved in getting ready for college, and I'll be starting on my senior year in high school. Oakley will be going with Brock, but Bobby couldn't get in. He'll be going to Junior College and hopes to be able to transfer after two years, assuming he still wants to by then.

Today is the same kind of day it was when I said goodbye to Joe. It's hot and golden out and some of the summer people have already begun to leave. The field by the house is full of tall goldenrod, still new and greenish, and black-eyed Susans, and Queen Anne's lace. Donald is waddling around catching grasshoppers. She's very white against the green, very clean-looking, and her bill is very bright orange. When a plane flies over she cocks her head to one side to look up at the sky.

It's funny, I've been working on this thing so long now that I'm sitting here at my desk wondering what to do next. In a way the truth has set me free; I've stopped having nightmares about the murder, and waking up with my insides cold and shivering. As I wrote about them the tears on the stranger's face became less touching, and now the stranger's face has faded out; I can no longer remember it. It used to be that it would occur to me from time to time and I'd shudder and have to say to whoever I was with, "A goose must have walked over my grave."

So I'm free. Writing this *did* work as I'd hoped. The only trouble is that Joe's face has dimmed out too, and finally I've really lost him. I used to have a sense of him inside me, sort of like a presence in the back corner of my mind—but he's gone now, all put down on paper. And I feel very lonely. Almost lonely enough to cry.

Writing this has changed me. I look up from my pile of manuscript and everything is different, or, rather, things look different to me—I'm the only thing that has changed.

After Joe killed the stranger I used to wish sometimes that Bonnie and Joe's son would come to see Joe, and I'd imagine a happy reunion with all the trimmings, and imagine showing Joe's son around and taking him out in the dory and all. Other times I used to be glad that Bonnie never showed up because, to be honest about it, I didn't want the competition. I didn't want anybody else playing Beauty to Joe's Beast. Then I'd be sorry about being so selfish, and want Joe to be happy and wonder why Bonnie never came to see him, even once.

It said in the paper that Joe had left his house and everything to Bonnie and the boy, and I spent a couple of months bracing myself to meet them; sometimes I wanted to because I was curious, and sometimes I didn't want to because I was afraid of being disappointed (if Bonnie had turned out to be ordinary it would have been awful). But she never came and in due time Mr. O'Connor put up a For Sale sign and began showing people the house. It hasn't been sold yet, but an architect is interested in it.

Yesterday I went down to the village and happened to run into Mr. Felcon on the street. Adonis was killed by a car this summer, but Mr. Felcon is still pursued by him, and still glances nervously over his shoulder and backs up to walls to talk to people. Mr. Felcon looked very small and shrivelled and, in fact, I discover that now he's several inches shorter than I am, even in his elevator shoes.

A funny thing happened. Usually Mr. Felcon grabs anyone he can get close enough to to catch and corners them and starts one of his speeches, but this time, feeling somehow sorry for him, I didn't dodge him when he came up, but smiled and said, "Good afternoon."

I thought I was letting myself in for a "Jesus is sad" spiel, but Mr. Felcon looked up in my face, got all confused, mumbled "Afternoon," and escaped (that's the only word for it). He ran away from me and disappeared into the nearest store.

I wondered what he saw in my face that frightened him so. Was it that he saw how small he is? Or did he see that I pity him? I can see now that Mom is right, it's tragic when a man becomes so much less than he might have been and should have been. It isn't funny when a human being becomes a caricature, because to become a caricature is to become less than human—a comic undertaker, an inexperienced shoplifter, a hypocritical preacher, a scrawny undersized creature scuttling down the street still pursued by the ghost of a dead dog. I wonder, was he afraid of me because I looked at him as if he was a person? Has he become so accustomed to his own caricature that he can't stand someone seeing through it? That indeed would be tragedy.

I saw Mrs. Root through the shop window and somehow she's no longer a wicked queen, but a woman who used to be handsome, fighting a losing battle against time and old age. Now I know what she and Mr. Felcon see in each other. She makes him important, and he makes her young. It seems very sad that there are people in the world that have so little.

It makes me feel very strange to know that there's nobody in my world to be frightened of any more, not the gossips, nor Miss Banner, nor anybody else. All the ogres have turned into stone in the sunlight. But if the world is less frightening, it is also sadder, because seeing it from other points of view, I begin to see how unhappy some people are.

It made me feel so queer that I went to the bakery to buy a bun. Nobody else was there so Mrs. Cellier asked me if I'd like some quince jam on it. Of course I said, "Yes." Sitting on the seawall eating the bun I felt a lot better. Even if the ogres are gone, and the people I'd thought of as frightening turned out to be sad instead, at least nice people like Mrs. Cellier were even realler and rounder and nicer than before, because now I can see her as a person, a happy, kind, warm, motherly person, instead of a dispenser of buns and butter and jam.

I showed this to Mom and Dad and Brock. Mom hadn't guessed anything, she said. I'd hoped for some kind of verdict from Mom and Dad as to if we'd done right in not telling. Dad tended to agree with Brock, but he ended up saying he couldn't really say one way or the other. Mom said, "Blessed are the merciful . . ." which it all well and good, but not a whole lot of help. Brock said he was glad anyway that he knew why I'd turned on him like that but he wished I'd told him at the time.

Joe is buried in one of those enormous military cemeteries, the kind with the endless, precise rows of crosses, all identical. We passed it on the way to visit the college Brock will be going to, but nobody wanted to stop. All the crosses are alike and you can't grieve for all of them; it's the nearest thing to an unmarked grave that you can get, I think. The grass is so smooth and well-kept it looks as if nobody is buried there at all.

C. F. Griffin

*was born in Albany, New York. Her father,
who died when she was seven, was head of
the geology department at Williams College. Her mother is a classical archeologist.*

*She attended public school in the early
grades, later attended an Episcopalian parochial school in Florida. She was not a good
student and graduated with difficulty from
a college prep school in Massachusetts. She
went to Smith, flunked out, then went to
Bennington and flunked out. After getting
good grades for a year she was allowed
to matriculate in the School of General
Studies, Columbia University and eventually graduated with a B.S. in Creative
Writing.*

*While living in New York she met and
married her husband who was at that time
getting his M.A. in psychology from City
College, New York. Miss Griffin has worked
as a dictaphone-typist, a waitress, a salesclerk, and an editor at the A.M.A.*

*She now lives in Wilmette, Illinois, with
her husband and three children, Theodore,*

Judith, and Lucinda. She and her husband breed purebred Pembroke Welsh Corgis on a small scale and hope eventually to become a registered kennel. Her husband also hybredizes iris and corresponds all over the world for the Species Committee of the Aril Society International. Besides the corgis, they have a mother cat and goldfish. In the past they have had ducks, mice and flying squirrels, not to mention turtles and frogs and similarly short-lived pets.

C. F. Griffin is the author of three other novels: Not Without Love, Nobody's Brother, and Instead of Ashes, all of which, like The Impermanence of Heroes, were first published in England. Not Without Love has been translated into Italian under the title, Si, Ma Con Amore.

In speaking of her writing, Miss Griffin says, "I only can write when I feel like it. There are times when I don't write at all and others when I work night and day. I have no schedules." She wrote The Impermanence of Heroes while suffering an attack of nostalgia for the sea, which she had not seen for over ten years. As she says, "Lake Michigan, nice as it is, is the wrong color, does not smell right, and lacks fauna."